Lift My Eyes

LIFT MY EYES

Magdalen Dugan

ELM HILL

A Division of
HarperCollins Christian Publishing

www.elmhillbooks.com

Lift My Eyes

Published in Nashville, Tennessee, by Elm Hill, an imprint of Thomas Nelson. Elm Hill and Thomas Nelson are registered trademarks of HarperCollins Christian Publishing, Inc.

Elm Hill titles may be purchased in bulk for educational, business, fund-raising, or sales promotional use. For information, please e-mail SpecialMarkets@ThomasNelson.com.

Publisher's Note: This novel is a work of fiction. Names, characters, places, and incidents are either products of the author's imagination or used fictitiously. All characters are fictional, and any similarity to people living or dead is purely coincidental.

Library of Congress Cataloging-in-Publication Data

Library of Congress Control Number: 2018966236

ISBN 978-1-400308606 (Paperback)
ISBN 978-1-400308613 (Hardbound)
ISBN 978-1-400308620 (eBook)

For David , Zoe, and Peter,
the best of editors

January 1, 1923

Tata, Hungary

Weak winter light slants through the frosted window. So another year begins. This tale of my life drones on—I have lost the thread. I have been searching the flames of our small fire, but they offer no clues. The critics have told the world that I am depressed, as if this were my personal problem. They should be more observant—everyone is depressed now. How could we fail to be? They have gone to war again and this time it has been the entire world—rulers with their reasons seizing what does not belong to them, soldiers destroying millions upon millions of lives that do not belong to them. These are the facts, and I am a realist. Interpretations get confusing.

In the corner of this parlor stands the painting of a soldier and his horse, which I have been struggling to finish since last summer. The horse is good, I think. I sketched him from a stallion that lives here in a pasture of what was once my husband Ferenc's ancestral estate. He is a deep-black Nonius, muscular with a prominent bone structure. I am told that the Hungarian army rode many of this breed during the war. This noble creature has survived his battles and is taking a rest now, occasionally being used for light farmwork. I like to visit him, to watch him canter through the quiet, open pasture, to feed him a crab apple from my hand. I have named him Obsidian, and it was he who inspired the painting. He is still strong and alert, and watched me with interest as I sketched him, which has allowed me to capture his head in a forward position. Since I studied with Emile Van Marcke in Paris, I have enjoyed portraying animals that meet the viewer's gaze and seem to be walking out of the painting, into the third dimension. In this painting, we view both horse and soldier closely as they walk toward us side by side. The battle is just over. The horse is not wounded, but is lathered with sweat. His eyes retain the overly excited, almost wild look an intelligent animal can express when under extreme stress. His posture is tense as he walks away from the danger he has just braved out of loyalty to his master. Yes, I think the horse is good.

It is the soldier who is the problem. I have no relationship with this particular soldier, but he repels me. He wears the uniform of the Hungarian army, which means that he has fought to protect my husband's homeland, the country that has received me in exile, but has he? He has almost certainly been conscripted to fight, as it is said that nine million Hungarians were. If this is so, he has not chosen either good or evil, but has simply done what he was told, and his is not a position with which I am sympathetic. On the other hand, it is possible that he has enlisted out of romantic ignorance, bewitched by the glamor of uniforms and weaponry, the reassurance of comrades and marching music, the dream of glory. Such a young soldier, though he is tragically mistaken, could be sincere. Do we not all want to become more than what we are? But then again, I tell myself, he may be not only naïve, but twisted in his heart, not caring that he kills, even liking to kill. People are complex creatures, and soldiers, I think, are no exception.

I have not been able to complete the face of the soldier because I do not know him as I know the horse. I do not really want to know him. I have seen too many soldiers. But I need, though I do not want, to know him. I cannot paint what I do not understand, and I need to paint this soldier who is every soldier. If I can know him well enough to paint him, perhaps I will understand.

I do not try to understand the causes and effects of this war, or any war, the way my husband and his friends continually try to do. I leave it to others to analyze political issues. I paint people and animals, and it is they I try to understand. The people who have engineered the conflict appear to me to have simple, hateful motives—greed, pride, anger. I do not want to paint them. The soldiers' motives are much more elusive. Their job is to kill and to be killed, but I do not know why they would agree to such a job, and I do not think most of them know, either.

The city of Tata has erected a memorial in the square, engraving on the granite base the names of hundreds from this small community alone who have perished. Their mothers, wives, and children visit the monument to honor their loved ones, to keep them in memory, but I do not think they understand what has happened. I have seen them standing there speechless, their hands hanging helplessly at their sides, looking up with blank faces at the monument, a bronze of a young soldier. If he had been sculpted differently, he might immortalize the flesh and breath of men they have lost, but the sculpture fails to inspire. He is not standing to proclaim a noble victory. Instead he has fallen and lies on the ground, raising only head and torso, as if with his last strength, to lift a bugle to his lips—a message to those who study war?

If only I could talk with Papa, I might be able to understand.

June 1864
(Sixty-one years earlier)

Franklin, Tennessee

Papa is preparing the wood for a piano. I stand behind him on tiptoes, watching as he smooths the surface with his plane, the muscles in his back standing up like ropes from the effort. Papa is a slim, strong man with light-brown hair that curls around his neck and ears. Its gold and red streaks catch the sun. He is the center of my world, and whatever I do during the day, I keep returning to him. When he looks up at me, light shines from the blueness of his eyes and we don't need to say anything because I know he loves me and I love him.

Papa is an artist, a master woodworker. He says he is fortunate to work with his body as well as his heart. He says an artist is someone who shows people the beauty that is all around us, beauty they might not have noticed. I always see beauty when I am with Papa. Today he is using a new wood for a special piano. Its grain alternates gold, brown, and red, like the strands of his hair in the sun.

"Papa, what is this wood with all the colors? I have never seen it before."

"This is rosewood, my Matilda. It is like the rosewood in our garden, but you have never seen the inside of the big branches. This is how rose branches look inside. And this is a special kind of rosewood that my customer shipped all the way from a country in South America called Brazil."

South America. Brazil. I ponder the sounds of the unfamiliar names. I am used to Papa talking about places of which I have no knowledge—Saxony where he was raised, New Orleans where he immigrated after finishing the training in his guild. The farthest I have travelled from Franklin, Tennessee, is to the neighboring towns where he takes me on rare occasions to deliver furniture. Once we travelled as far as Nashville, a city so large and busy I remember it only as impressions of tall buildings, rattling carriages, and strange new smells all mixed together. I am content in the small, secure world of our family home, and as yet I have no desire to wander.

Papa lays down his plane, takes my tiny hand in his large, work-roughened hand, and strokes it across the satiny surface of the wood. It feels like the wondrous black walnut bannister of our staircase, a single piece of wood that Papa has made to curve and turn all the way from the first floor of our house to the second. The bannister wood feels like it is still alive because it holds heat or cold from the air. Today, in the late morning sun, the rosewood is warmer than my hand. I stroke it, and then stroke Papa's soft brown beard.

"Shall I sand the wood now, Tillie? What do you say?"

I nod, and soon a delicious fragrance arises. Struck by a new idea, I run to the garden to smell first one rose and then another, each variety similar to yet unique from the others, as I have long known. Now I marvel that the wood scent is like them all in sweetness but unlike them because it is richer and deeper. I break off a stem from a bush of hearty red roses and inhale—yes, something like Papa's wood.

As I loved to do then, I take the stick and trace in the dry soil, outlining, erasing, outlining again the images of a bloom, a woody stem, a piece of cut wood, a rosewood piano.

I do not yet have the words, but that morning just a few months before the battle, I sense, more deeply than thoughts or words, how all living things belong to each other. This is what I will always want to draw.

*****

January 1, 1923

Tata, Hungary

But however will I draw this soldier as belonging to all of us? I do not know how to bring this grieving to its conclusion.

My parents' sober, noble faces watch me from the miniatures on our mantelpiece, challenging me to recover from tragedy and disaster as they always did.

Nearly sixty years ago, just after the Civil War battle that changed the course of our family's lives, Papa entered the devastated hallway of the home that he had built with his own hands. He clutched the box of precious woodworking tools he had managed to save from the pillage of our property, the pillage that our enemies required for the purpose of killing our neighbors. He surveyed the scene in silence, and bowed his head for a long moment. When he raised it again, he told us, "We have our lives. We have each other. Now we will rebuild."

Was he not angry over all the life and beauty they took from us, all that could never be recovered? I did not have the words to ask him then—their war had literally stolen my voice and it was months before I could find it again. I could not tell him how I hated them. I could not remind him that they had even stolen some of us from each other.

Mama used to have a ruby and gold vase that she had brought to Tennessee all the way from Bavaria. The year before the battle, when I was five years old, I was holding the faceted crystal to a candle flame, turning it this way and that as it split the light into hundreds of pieces and cast it across the dining room walls. Suddenly the precious object slipped from my hands and shattered at my feet.

"Mama! Your treasure!" I cried. If it had been my favorite porcelain doll lying at my feet in pieces, I would not have been more upset.

Mama took my face between her warm, strong hands and smiled with her eyes. "Hush, little one. It is only a thing. You are the treasure, Matilda."

Then she was weeping, and left the room. Papa lifted me to his knee.

"Your Mama is not upset about the broken vase, Tillie. She has lost two of her true treasures, Julian and Julia."

Earlier that year, my two-year-old twin brother and sister had run from the backyard to the stream in the woods and drunk the water. When Mama reached them, they were holding their stomachs and vomiting. Union soldiers had poisoned the stream in anticipation of a battle, but there was no battle in Franklin, Tennessee, that year. There were only two dead babies laid out on our dining table like perfect porcelain dolls.

*****

December 3, 1864
(Sixty years earlier)

Franklin, TN

We are in the Carters' parlor for Tod Carter's funeral. It feels so different from the room of our last visit here only weeks ago. The drawn curtains enclose us in a dark sadness. Black cloths cover the mirrors, silencing everyone. In the middle of the room, Tod's body lies on a table with some holly laid around him. It is frighteningly still.

Last night, Papa explained what happened. Tod died yesterday from wounds he received in the battle two days before. At first the family couldn't find him and went out to search the terrible fields of death. His sisters found him badly wounded—the rest of the family knew by their screams that they had found him. Some soldiers carried him into his house, wrapped in an overcoat. Dr. Roberts came to take care of him, but there wasn't much he could do. They knew he was going to die, though he was able to talk with his family for a while first. They were able to say good-bye.

I wish I could have said good-bye to him. I would have kissed his cheek the way I used to when he was alive, when his whiskers tickled my lips and he smelled like soap and tobacco. Some of his family has gone up to kiss him. I am afraid to kiss him now.

Mr. Carter says Tod did not have to fight because he was a quartermaster. That's a soldier who takes care of the other soldiers. Tod did not have to fight, but I know he wanted to help; he always wanted to help. He rode into the battle crying out, "Follow me, boys. I'm almost home." But a bullet hit him as he was almost at his home, and he couldn't walk by himself anymore. The blue soldiers killed him and I will not forgive them.

Why can I not cry? Mrs. Carter is crying so much they have to take her out for a while. I just keep thinking it is so strange to look at him lying there, when only a few days ago he was telling me I was his sweetheart and swinging me through the air. I guess I did not really believe that he would wait for me and marry me because he is—he was—a big man and I am a little girl, but I did know he liked me and I liked him. Now he is gone, and only this too-still body is left.

Everyone has brought what food they have left from the raiding of the blue soldiers, and after we pray for Tod to be at peace we eat together, but no one talks much. No one but my family seems to notice that I cannot speak, not at all. We are all together in the same bad dream.

*****

January 1, 1923

Tata, Hungary

I have drawn as close to the fire as I can without scorching my skirts. Life here in Tata is difficult at any time, but in winter it is nearly impossible. Though wrapped in wool from the outside in, even to my woolen stockings, I cannot fend off the damp cold. My muscles are tightened with it and will not let go. The outdoor thermometer has read below zero for more than a month, and the constantly falling wet snow soon hardens to ice, sealing us inside this house like insects in amber. We spend most of our day in this parlor where we can afford to keep a fire burning. Several times a day I venture to the kitchen to make tea or prepare some soup. At night we return to the cocoon of our bedroom and the oblivion of sleep. So it has been, day after day, for each of the eight winters we have lived here.

My husband Ferenc reaches to take my free hand. Though he is aging as I am, and though his country is crumbling around him, he is still every inch the nobleman—sitting erect in his wing chair, pipe in hand, perusing the newspaper. In the ten years we have been married, his hair, which he wears long to his jawline, has taken on a hue of vigorous iron grey. As he turns to smile at me, the tanned skin of his face creases like fine leather and his hand, as he holds mine, has the supple softness of my Florentine kidskin gloves. My hand rests in his as if in a glove, snugly, comfortingly.

Ferenc often teases me about having to sit to my left if he hopes to capture my hand, since my right hand is always busy sketching or writing. Although I do not have great energy for either today, the potential this new year offers compels me to try. I will not paint today, though. I am not ready. I need to consider how to make an end of what has been so that I can begin again. The cycle of life requires it.

The Great War has been over for more than two years, but I have not been able to make an end of it. A million of this country's soldiers are dead, and many more are missing in action. In Tata, scarcely a household has escaped tragedy. Most of those who have returned are missing parts—legs, arms, minds, the will to live. This small community has had its life sucked from it, and it is no doubt the same everywhere.

For nearly eight years we have been hungry—some dangerously so, some, like me, only annoyingly so. I eat enough to sustain myself—bread, soup, an egg when one is available. Since the blockade of food has been lifted and the soldiers have come home to farm again we have better food with more variety, but over the past years I have learned to eat little. I must not complain. Often, as I serve soup to the townspeople, I look into the wan faces and sunken eyes of those far hungrier than I.

The truth is that I am ashamed to be so miserable. My husband is alive, whole, and at my side. I am not starving; I am not without shelter. I am free to paint as much as strength allows. But I am still very, very angry. What right did they have to set the world to killing one another?

I am shivering now, and must wrap the blankets more closely around my legs and shoulders. As he reads the newspaper, Ferenc once in a while comments aloud on world events, which, for some reason, still interest him. The empire that was once his heritage is splintered into more than a dozen pieces, which still, postwar, are being invaded by enemies and infiltrated by agitators wanting revolution. Evidently Russia has formed a "Soviet Union," and what that will mean to us here in what is left of Hungary is something he tries to imagine.

I do not trust any of them—the heads of state, the princes, the sons of men. They have taken nearly everything of value, though they cannot completely take us from each other as long as we can remember.

And what is there to do today in Tata, Hungary, at sixty-five years old, in the depth of winter, in the depth of exile, except to remember? Moments of my life are flashing through my thoughts like the images of a kaleidoscope—light, patterns, colors—a bright, fragmented panorama.

*****

November 29, 1864 (Four days before the battle)

Franklin, Tennessee

Running down the stairs, I pass my palm along the cool smoothness of the bannister Papa has made. I swing around the corner and into the dining room, which holds even more wonders than I have been imagining all this week as I have waited for today. Mama and Amelia have baked me a cake, and displayed it on a tall glass stand. It is decorated with white butter frosting and clusters of red gooseberries. I know that inside that frosting I will find pieces of crunchy pecan and soft, sweet apple. More apples decorate the table, along with a pitcher brimming with Ute's creamy milk.

The whole family is here for my sixth birthday party. Papa sits at the head of the table, handsome in a dark-blue suit and a light-blue shirt that make his eyes look even bluer than usual. Mama is serving, standing tall over the table. She is a big, strong woman, almost as tall as Papa, with deep-set, golden-brown eyes. She has piled her curly brown hair on top of her head, and pulled some down into long tendrils that fall over her shoulders. When she is working indoors, she smells of bread dough and washing soap and lavender, but when she is working outdoors she smells of garden loam and pasture grass.

My brother Joseph, who has finished high school and gone to work in Nashville, has returned just for my party, and Tod Carter, our neighbors' son, has taken leave from the Confederate Army to visit his family and Joseph. Tod is a Confederate soldier, but he is not dressed in his gray uniform today. He says he can stay only a few hours, because the Yankees are occupying our town and may cause him trouble if they find him. He always talks about how he is loyal to the Confederacy to the death, how he would do anything to protect his home and his way of life. Today he is arguing with Joseph for refusing to take a side in the war.

"Look, Lotz, I know you are not a coward, but it has to look that way to people who don't know you."

"People can think what they like. My father does not take a side, and it is clear that he is not a coward," Joseph answers.

"He certainly is not. My apologies, Mr. Lotz. I would never imply such a thing. But, Joe, even though your family is Bavarian, you grew up here. You are a Tennessean."

"The United States is my country, not Tennessee or the North or the South but the whole country. This is not my battle you all are fighting."

Then Tod pretends to be mad. He punches Joseph in the arm and wrestles with him a little before they slap each other on the back and drink some punch. Joseph and Tod grew up together and are almost brothers.

Though of course he has come to see his friend, Tod insists that he is here particularly to see me because I am his girl. He has brought me a tiny toy wagon carved of wood, drawn by a perfect wooden ox with delicate horns curving from its bowed head.

"Did you carve this, Tod?" I ask, cradling his gift in my cupped palms.

"I sure did. I made it for my girl. You are still my girl, aren't you, Tillie? Or have you gotten too old to be interested in a young fella like me?"

I laugh, and everyone laughs, and Tod lifts me by the shoulders and spins me in a circle so that the skirt of my blue wool dress bells out around me.

"This may be Tennessee, but you look just like a Virginia bluebell, Miss Tillie," he says, returning me to my feet and bowing.

Joseph has also made a gift, a braided leather leash, to lead my pet calf Mattie. But the best gift of all comes from Papa and Mama—a tablet of paper and a set of Faber pencils.

"You have done well with your stick drawings, my Tillie," Papa says. "It is time now to draw some pictures you can keep."

He lays his hand on my head as if blessing me, and his hand is warm and kind. Mama's eyes smile in the silent way she has, and I know she is proud of me. I get up from the table to hug first Papa, then Mama. Paul and I exchange excited glances, and he mouths the words, "Tomorrow morning." My brother Paul is nine, just old enough to protect and help me. He is my best friend. We are always drawing together, and now, when we have perfected a stick drawing, we will be able to transfer it to the precious new paper. I know what the subject of this first drawing will be—Mattie, my pet calf.

*****

April 1864

(Seven months earlier)

Franklin, Tennessee

"Go ahead, Matilda. Don't be shy," my brother Joseph urges me, patting my shoulder.

Joseph is my hero, nearly a man already, just about to finish high school with honors and go out into the world.

"This is your calf, Matilda. Papa said she could be. So you have to name her," he insists.

We have watched as our milk cow Ute has birthed a little wet lump of pink flesh that looks barely alive. Besides Joseph, my big sister Amelia is here, and my closest brother Paul. Our baby brother Augustus, "Gus," is only three and has not been admitted to this important event. During the birth, Ute bellowed fiercely for the longest time, and finally the small, sweet creature dropped. We have stayed here while the pink lump found her feet and teetered onto her wobbly legs to drink from Ute's teat.

At five years old, I feel very grown up to be allowed to watch this wonder, and especially to know that Ute's calf will be my own pet. But what special name can I give her?

"Can I call her Tillie, like Papa calls me?"

"It isn't proper to call an animal after a person," Amelia says.

Amelia is already seventeen and she is always saying things like this, much more often than Mama does. I want to tell her that she is not my mother, but I resist. The occasion is too special for a fight with Amelia. Besides, she can be kind sometimes, and when she plays the piano I could listen to her all day.

But I am baffled. I don't know many names that aren't names of people or towns or something I couldn't call a calf.

"W-e-l-l-l," says Joseph, never at a loss, "how about if we call her "Mattie"? That's the first part of your name, but no one calls you that, so Amelia can't object."

I throw my arms around Joseph's leg, and then scramble between the fence slats to pet my new calf and lay my cheek against her damp, warm side. "Hello, Mattie," I whisper into her moist ear. "You and I are going to be friends."

And we are. All through that last spring before the battle, Mattie and I run through the pastures together. Her rough tongue tickles my palm as I feed her with the greenest, most tender new grass. I like to roll down the grassy hill above the pasture where she grazes, and surprise her with a hug. Sometimes I climb up on her back and ride her through the pasture, until Amelia calls to me to get down before I break my neck. Most of the time I obey, though it doesn't seem so far to fall.

*****

November 30, 1864 (Seven months later, the day of the battle)

Franklin, Tennessee

I wake at sunrise and run to the window to take in the brilliant colors. I cannot wait to draw my first picture on paper, one I will be able to keep. It will be of my Mattie.

I dress quickly, shivering in the cold air. Grabbing my new pencils and tablet, I run down the stairs and out the back door. Mattie is standing in the pasture, nibbling grass, but when she sees me, she comes right up to the fence to lick my hands and face.

I begin to sketch her, first using a stick to draw in the bare earth along the fence line, the way I have always done with Paul. Her silky skin is white with patches of black; her deep, peaceful brown eyes are looking into mine. I try many sketches in the earth, and when Paul joins me, he corrects a line here, a curve there, until he finally agrees that I am ready to use the pencils and paper. But now I must learn an early lesson about the limits and challenges of each different medium, because pencil and paper work very differently from stick and earth. Especially, I must begin to learn about shading, showing light and shadow in ways impossible with the earthen sketches but necessary on paper. I must erase and begin again many times. After about two hours, Paul and I return to the house, hungry and a little frustrated.

That day I do not finish my first real drawing.

As we are eating our lunch, we hear something strange, look at each other, and jump up in alarm. From the Granny White turnpike, and eventually right in front of our house, comes a noise such as I have never heard before, as if all the people in the huge city of Nashville were in one small spot, talking all at once. We run out to the front yard, and I cannot believe my eyes—as far as I can see in both directions, the Pike is filled with blue uniforms.

These blue soldiers themselves are not a strange sight to me; some have been here since spring, though Papa and Mama always say they have no right to be here, no right to make the demands they do. I know that they killed our babies, and I already hate them, but up until now there have been only a few. This appearance today is something else entirely—a powerful river of blue that I know does not mean us any good. My stomach feels sick and I think I might lose my lunch. And then, some of them walk right up to our porch and knock on the door. Paul and I crouch down at the side of the house, where we can hear them but they cannot see us. Papa answers the door.

"Are you the owner of this property?" a Yankee soldier demands of Papa.

"I am. I am Johann Albert Lotz, and this is my house."

"By order of Major General Schofield, my men are occupying your land."

"For what possible purpose?"

"We need a base and provisions. We will also need wood for a battlement."

"But my family—"

"We will not harm your family, Mr. Lotz."

They talk some more, and Papa sounds very upset, but in the end the blue uniforms begin to swarm over our yard. Papa calls us all inside, and I watch from the back windows as they tear down our barn, our stable, our kitchen house, and all the other buildings except our house itself. They even tear down Papa's woodworking shop, though Papa pleads with them to spare it for our livelihood. Then to all our horror, they cut down our trees, every one of them—the cedar that smelled like perfume every time Papa cut branches to make chests, the dogwood that burst into white blooms in spring, even the huge old oak we played under in the summertime, where Paul and I would lean against the trunk as thick as a wall and look at picture books, all fallen to the ground and hacked to pieces so that the land is not our yard any longer.

Worse than all of this, with guns and swords and bayonets they kill our animals—our eight hogs and our twelve sheep and our whole flock of chickens. The grass is red with blood. The death sounds of that slaughter are not like those of hog-killing in the fall, when Papa takes an animal or two that we will need for winter meat. This is an hour of total devastation, with scarcely a creature left standing. While Amelia and I hold each other and cry, they even kill gentle, good Ute, who does not even know to resist, but stands there patiently as they shoot her in the head.

Papa has told us we must stay inside, but when they shoot Ute, I know that the unthinkable could happen, and I run out the back door before anyone can stop me, run as fast as I can toward the pasture where I left little Mattie only a few hours before. As accustomed as I am to obeying Mama, when she calls after me, I do not even turn around.

But before I reach the pasture, I can see that it is too late. Mattie is lying on her side, bleeding from her head. I run to cradle her poor head in my lap. She is lowing miserably, her eyes seeming to search mine for an answer to why this is happening. I stroke her sides. Her blood reddens my hands and arms, soaks into my skirt. We sit like this for a very long time until she goes silent, and then limp.

It is as if I were watching all of this, and not experiencing it myself. A girl, all covered with blood, is holding in her lap a dead calf, her pet, her special friend. It is sad.

A blue uniform with a face watches me, approaches me, and begins to speak. At first I do not hear what he is saying, though his mouth is moving. Eventually I register bits and pieces of his words.

"Sorry, little girl… I did not mean to...got carried away…tired and hungry…following orders…daughter about your age…"

To my surprise and horror, this hand that has killed Mattie is reaching toward me, is about to touch me. I jump to my feet, wrenched from sorrow by another feeling I do not understand, one that seizes me strongly, shakes my body.

"Do not touch me! I hate you. You are bad. You kill everything. You steal and destroy everything. Go away! Go away right now and leave us alone!"

The man looks down at the ground and then turns back to the slaughter. Not until he has gone do I cry. I cry until I am too exhausted to cry anymore. But this is only the preparation for what is to come.

*****

NOVEMBER 30, 1864 (LATER THAT DAY, AROUND DUSK)

Franklin, Tennessee

Amelia is chopping vegetables for supper. I wonder how any of us will be able to eat—I still feel like I am going to vomit. The blue uniforms are all eating, though—hunched around their open fires fueled by our felled trees, devouring the hogs that were meant to feed us throughout the winter, devouring Ute, devouring Mattie.

Mama enters the kitchen in her coat and hat. The daylight is fading, so I wonder where she can be going.

"*Kommt jetzt!*"

She is telling us all to come with her right away. Her voice is calm and steady, but Mama normally speaks English, and when she speaks German, we know that she is very serious. Amelia promptly lays down her knife, unties her apron, and takes her coat from the peg near the kitchen door.

"Do I have to come right now?" Paul asks. He has been sketching the devastation of our backyard, and I know that he is hurrying to finish before he loses the light. This drawing seems to make him feel better somehow. I cannot look out there anymore, but I have been watching him as he works, his right hand making sure, swift strokes across the paper, his left raised from time to time to check perspective, his brow crinkled in concentration. He is drawing tree stumps, hacked branches, men in blue uniforms with dark, menacing faces gnawing on bones.

"*Ja stimmt! Jetzt, Paul!*" Mama answers.

Paul does not mistake her tone this time, and leaps to put on his coat. Mama takes my hand in her strong, sure hand. In the hall, we join Papa, who grips his toolbox with one hand, and with the other clasps sleeping baby Gus to his shoulder. Mama and Papa look at each other wordlessly. I am with them, so I am not afraid, but I know that we are on guard, as a family of deer who sense a hunter will stand listening for a moment before they flee.

*****

November 30, 1864

(The night of that same day)

Franklin, Tennessee

We are huddled in the Carters' storage cellar, starting at the reports of the guns cracking over our heads, shaking with the thunder of the canon. Earlier today, as the grey uniforms streamed up Columbia Pike to meet the blue ones, Papa brought us here to our neighbors' home to seek shelter. Papa has kept us here, so I believe that all will be well.

All of the Carter family is here, except Tod who they say is out there with the Confederate Army. All of our family is here, except for Joseph, who returned to his work in Nashville early yesterday, before the soldiers arrived. Mama says Joseph was sent away by the powers above to be spared from all this, and that our twins, Julian and Julius who died last year, have been spared this, as well.

Mama has not been spared. As she speaks of her dead babies her eyes, usually golden brown like honey, darken with grief, and her wide mouth pulls tight as it does when she is choosing not to weep. Gus is asleep at the ample pillow of one of her breasts, but I scramble up to her other side, making sure to keep my wet skirts away from her. I throw my arms around her neck, and rest my head over her heart.

"I hate them, Mama."

"No, Tillie, you mustn't."

"I do, though. I hate the blue uniforms. They killed our babies. They killed Mattie and Ute. They kill and steal and make everything ugly."

"Tillie, dear, hating will only hurt your own heart. You are very young, and it is hard for you to understand this, but most people are doing what they think is good, even when that harms other people. That is what is happening out there right now. Yankee soldiers are killing Confederate soldiers, and Confederate soldiers are killing Yankee soldiers. It is horrible, and it is sad, and it is hurting so many people, but if we asked them right now, most of them would say that what they are doing is good."

"Was it good that they killed Julian and Julius?"

"Dear child, of course it was not good, but the Yankee soldiers did not intend to kill our babies. They did not even think about them, or about any of us who were just trying to live in our home. They were doing their jobs—horrible jobs of killing people who think differently than they do."

"That is what the blue uniform was telling me, Mama. They didn't mean to kill Mattie. Somebody made a mistake. But, Mama, one minute there was her sweet life and the next minute there was not. I cannot stop hating them."

Mama holds me closer and whispers, "You are hurting badly right now, Tillie. It may take you a while to forgive."

I do not want to forgive the blue uniforms, though I do not say this to Mama. Every time I think about them I get the same shaking feeling I had with the soldier who shot Mattie. My stomach pulls together inside and I want to scream.

It is different for Mama. Mama is stronger than anybody, even stronger than Papa, I think. Papa is the sky—high and full of light with all sorts of bright beauty shining from him. But Mama is the earth that holds us up and feeds us and never changes. I know that we all came from her as Mattie came from Ute—Paul, and Gus and I, and also Amelia and Joseph a long time ago when Mama was married to another man in Bavaria. What a great woman she is—a tall and solid woman in black silk dresses with full skirts that Paul and Gus and I hide beneath when we are playing. And the heart in her is great, great enough to forgive these people who take so much from us.

The heart in me is little and it hurts.

Now the blue uniforms throw open the door of the cellar. Mr. Carter jumps to his feet and meets them at the door.

"We are going to fire from this room now," one of the uniforms says.

"Indeed you are not, sir," answers Mr. Carter. "You have already moved us from the lower dining room where the ladies could sit on chairs and where there was at least a carpet for the rest of us. Now we are in a damp, drafty storage space, sitting upon cement. There is no lower room remaining that you have not occupied. Where would you have us go?"

"Well, you will just need to go upstairs—"

Papa rises and joins Mr. Carter at the door so that their bodies stand between their families and the blue uniforms. It is hard for me to breathe. Will they kill us, too? Or put us in a place where the bullets will kill us? Papa's face is sterner than I have ever seen it.

"My good sir," Papa says, "your commanding officer vowed to me that my family would not be harmed. Now you are asking us to bring our wives and children into rooms where bullets are most certainly penetrating the walls. We shall not do as you ask."

"This is not a discussion!" The blue uniform is yelling now, spit flying from his mouth. "This is an order! We are in the midst of a battle and you are on the opposing side!"

"In fact, sir, I am not on the opposing side. I am a civilian, an

American citizen, who is not on either side. I am simply trying to keep my wife and children safe."

This seems to confuse the blue uniform enough to silence him, and he leaves. Papa and Mr. Carter do not move from the doorway. The one who comes next is better dressed, and speaks more politely.

"Good evening, Mr. Carter, Mr. Lotz. We are sorry to trouble you, but my men need to fire from this room and you will need to move."

"Good evening, Commander Schofield," Mr. Carter replies. "Have your men finished firing from the other lower rooms?"

"They have not."

"I see. Then where would you move our wives and children, Commander? Surely you are not suggesting that they shelter in upper rooms, which are being penetrated by bullets and cannon as we speak?"

"We have no choice, sir."

"You, among all your army, are the one who does have a choice, Commander," says Papa. "You will remember your promise that our families would be safe."

The blue commander looks at his boots, looks up, nods, and leaves. He does not return, but I was so afraid that he would shoot Papa that I started shaking, and now I cannot stop and my skirts are wet because when I asked Amelia hours ago where I could use the toilet she just shook her head and then Papa was standing in front of the blue commander and his gun. Afterward, everyone says that Mr. Carter and Papa saved our lives.

I smell bad. I want to wash. I am hungry. I am tired, so tired, but the shrieks of men and the braying of horses, the thunder of cannons and the crack of rifles keep us from sleep. Even worse than my own bad smell is the reek of blood and burning coming from outside.

"Is this hell?" Gus asks through tears, his little face full of fear.

"No, child. We are near something like hell, but you are safe," Mama answers.

Mama holds Gus closer and rocks him. She has held him all through this horrible night, rocking him and humming to him, trying, usually unsuccessfully, to stop his crying. But when he dozes off, she reaches out and puts her hand on my head.

"Try to sleep, Matilda," she says.

I want to tell her that it is impossible to sleep, that the noise is painful, that my ears are ringing so loudly that I can hardly hear her speaking to me. I want to tell her that I am afraid to close my eyes, that I am still shivering, that I want to cry—but I cannot speak now.

I grab Mama's arm, open my mouth, and try again—no sound.

"Matilda? Are you choking?" Mama lays Gus on Amelia's lap and slaps my back. She takes me by the shoulders and observes me. I shake my head. I clap my hands to my ears and open my mouth as if screaming, to show her that there is a ringing in my head and that no sound can come from my mouth. That I am not choking. That I cannot speak. I cannot speak at all.

*****

December 1, 1864
(The next day)
Franklin, Tennessee

After the longest wait I can remember—nineteen hours, as I learn later—Papa goes upstairs and returns to tell us we can go home. Amelia hands Augustus to Papa and Mama, who has held and comforted me for hours now, stands to cradle me as if I were still a baby. Since Gus was born, she has not carried me. Her arms feel wonderfully safe. I put my face against her soft, firm cheek. We begin to climb the stairs. Before we reach the porch, she takes my face in one muscular hand and looks into my eyes.

"Listen to me, Matilda, listen very carefully."

I nod. I listen.

"Do you remember the song we sing with Amelia sometimes, 'Lift thine eyes, O lift thine eyes'?"

I nod again.

"Good, child. I want you to lift your eyes now, Matilda. Look up, up into the hills, and into the sky. You must not look down. You must not see such a sight as you would see if you looked down. Will you do as I say?"

I nod once more. Still my ears make a loud ringing and I cannot speak. I look up. There are hardly any more treetops. There is gray smoke, and the air stinks of burning and blood, like meat. But my eyes find the hills through the smoke. The snow at their tops still looks clean and fresh.

Mama walks very, very slowly, with jerking movements as if she is climbing over logs. Sometimes she trips and grips me closely, but she keeps her balance and we do not fall. As we walk she sings. "Lift thine eyes, O lift thine eyes to the mountains, whence cometh help." I want to sing with her, to help her rich and lonely voice to fill this place that is so horrible that I am not allowed to look at it. But I simply hug Mama more closely, and she sings even more loudly. "He hath said, thy foot shall not be moved. Thy Keeper will never slumber."

I wonder that it can be taking so long to get home, when home is only across the street from the Carters'. I start to look down at Mama's face to see what the matter is, but she has my head in her palm, and turns it back to the sky.

"Do you remember the story of Orpheus and Eurydice, Tillie?"

I nod. I love to listen to the myths Mama reads me, and this is one of my favorites, though it is very sad. Orpheus loved his wife Eurydice very much but she died and went to Hades which is like hell, and he played the harp so beautifully that the Hades god let her leave. Then in one moment Orpheus looked back and lost her forever.

"It was so very important for Orpheus not to look back, Tillie. Let's pretend you are Orpheus and we are escaping from Hades, for indeed we are. Only you must look up instead of forward. Can you do that, my Tillie? Tillie?"

She understands that I have lost my voice, but I have to answer somehow, so I pat her cheek.

"Good girl, Tillie. It is just a little longer." Again she begins to sing.

Orpheus forgot his promise for just a moment and so he looked back. I cannot make such a mistake. I arch my neck and look higher. Ravens are flying in a circle above us the way they do above animals that die in a field. The burning smell catches at the back of my throat and makes my stomach want to vomit, but there is nothing there to vomit now. Mama walks even more slowly, with greater jerking and more tripping, and holds me very tightly. My neck aches, but I will not look down.

At last Mama says, "We are just in front of our house, Matilda."

She has spoken too soon. When I lower my eyes to our front yard the first thing I see is a wonderful drum. I think that maybe we can keep it and Paul and I can play with it. But then, lying near the drum, I see the one who must have played it—the little boy dressed in blue, not much bigger than I am, lying so still, too still, still as a stone.

*****

December 1864 (The next week)

Franklin, Tennessee

Our family has returned, but it is not to the home Papa built for us, not to the home he showed his customers so they could see his beautiful woodworking. That home, which I will always remember, is gone forever.

A cannonball has crashed through the roof and the upstairs floor and all the way into the parlor, destroying the wonderful piano with the carvings of plums and apples. All the windows in the library and dining room are smashed now, with jagged, dirty teeth of glass jutting from their frames. Bullets have bitten through the walls. Worst of all, the staircase has crashed down—the lovely bannister lying all broken and splintered in the hallway. I look and look, but still I cannot believe it. Thankfully, the roaring and ringing in my ears is less now, but still I cannot cry or speak, though Mama has heated water over an open fire in the yard and calmed my shaking with a warm bath, warm soup, and blankets.

The first day back home and some days afterward are brisk with tasks to accomplish and people to help. Mama hangs a red flag from the porch; she tells us this is so everyone knows that we can tend the wounded here. And we do—so very many of them, a confusion of gray and blue—and a confusion of feelings about the two. It is not only the Yankees who have hurt and killed—the Confederate soldiers have, too, Papa reminds us. Now men who were trying to kill each other only a day ago lie side by side in pain, and it is our duty to care for them without partiality. Mama and Amelia do as he says. I am glad I am little and do not have to help any of these soldiers.

More strangers than I have ever seen walk into our house or are carried in on stretchers or blankets. They lean against the walls and sprawl on the floors, soaking our carpets with dark-red blood. When we run out of room in the house, they fill the back porch in spite of the bitter cold. There are never enough blankets, and we have pulled down draperies and pulled up rugs for coverings. Mama and Amelia do what they can, mostly trying to keep their wounds clean and make them more comfortable, they tell us when we all gather in the evenings. They give me jobs like tearing sheets for bandages and carrying basins of water for washing wounds. Some of the men moan and cry out, but most are silent and sad. Doctors come in and out to use the parlor for a surgery. Through the sometimes open door, I glimpse men bleeding on our dining table and our kitchen table. Most of the time, though, Mama keeps that door closed and tells me to stay with Papa and help him, but no matter where I am in the house and no matter how my ears still buzz as if a swarm of bees were caught inside them, I can still hear the screams from that room. Mama says the doctors have to do things that hurt the men, to keep them alive. Amelia says that these men are not the worst off, that the worst have been brought to Carnton Plantation, where there are more rooms for surgeries and where there are slaves to help. Papa and Mama have never kept a slave; they say that we need to work with our own hands for what we need.

Papa spends these first days of our changed life quickly fixing the worst of the damage to our house. When I am sent to help him, he lets me hold the boards in place while he hammers. Sometimes I fetch tools or nails. Papa's work is not beautiful now as it has always been before. As he works, he explains how he is trying to protect us from the cold. He nails boards over the holes where the windows were, and over the holes the bullets have made in the walls. He closes the holes in the roof and ceilings, to keep us dry and at least a little warmer. The side of the house where the library and dining room used to be—once my favorite part of our home, with sunlight streaming through its tall, wide windows—was directly exposed to the battle. It is all boarded up and dark now, so cold from the wind blowing through the small cracks between the boards that we cannot use it except to house the wounded who would otherwise have to lie on the porch.

During these days, I begin to understand that my sensitive artist Papa is badly wounded in his heart. While Mama seems no different from before, except for being busy every moment, Papa's light is dimmer than it used to be. He speaks little, and sighs often, instead of humming as he used to do. One day he lays down his tools to take me on his knee and stroke my hair.

"How are you getting along, little Tillie?"

I pat his soft beard and he puts his hand on mine.

"Do not be afraid that you cannot speak, Tillie. This has been a frightening time for you, with many difficult changes. Time and love will restore your voice. Will you remember that?"

I nod, looking into his sky-blue eyes and hoping that time and love will heal him, too.

Our family spends short, quiet evenings in the root cellar, wrapped in coats and blankets against the cold. Everyone says this is the coldest winter we have had in Franklin in ten years, and I have never been so very cold for such a long time. This is not the chill I have felt walking to church in winter with my toes and fingers tingling as I caught snowflakes on my tongue, and eventually sighing with the comfort of warmth and candlelight when we arrived. At night when the sun has set and we have stopped moving our bodies to work, this cold holds me in a tight grip all over my body, and it will not let go. Sometimes in the middle of the night when I am lying still, it shakes me so I cannot sleep, and when I do finally sleep, it continues to squeeze my arms and legs so hard that they ache the next morning. My throat is sore, and I cannot stop coughing.

During the past few days, it has begun to snow hard, and the wind whistles through any opening. Because our chimneys are broken, we cannot build any fires in the proper rooms, and of course there is no fireplace in the cellar. Papa has used bricks to seal the upstairs fireplaces and chimneys as much as possible. He promises that soon we will have coal fires in the downstairs rooms. For the time being, we spend a short time exchanging messages and eating our supper, and then retreat to makeshift beds until the sun rises.

We cannot go upstairs to the second floor yet because of the broken stairs, though from time to time Papa somehow manages to get up there to throw down clothes and blankets. On one of these occasions, he calls to me from above.

"Tillie, your china doll is safe in her cradle, but I cannot bring her downstairs because she could break so easily in all the confusion. I have something for you, though. Pile the blankets right here below me and stand back."

I obey, and I am rewarded by the sight of my leather horse Blackie, leaping safely from Papa's hand onto the blanket. I lift Blackie and hug him, and then make him gallop through the air toward Papa on high above us, to say thank you.

That night as we gather in the cellar, Papa speaks more than he has since the battle.

"Amelia, Paul, Matilda, you all show promise as artists, Amelia with piano and voice, Paul and Matilda with drawing and eventually painting. You know what it is to love beauty and to want to recreate it, to share it. The home we must live in now is not the work of art I created for you and your mother to enjoy. It is not the masterpiece I created to show to potential customers what a master woodworker can do so they would want to hire me. People who visited admired the carvings on our portico and finials and columns. They admired the ornaments carved into the furniture and marveled at how I was able to make such a staircase as ours from planks of wood, to shape its curves so perfectly. They said I was a genius with wood, but, though that pleased me, I had to correct them. I am not a genius, and you do not need to be geniuses. I am a simple man who has worked hard at his craft, and this is what you need to do, as well, no matter what befalls you, if you wish to make art.

"I will need to work harder now, and we will have much less than we did before. My masterpieces are destroyed—the piano, the mantelpieces, and even the staircase. I will not be able to replace any of these for a long time, if ever. My woodshop has been torn down. My lumber and even all our trees have been taken. Now only cheap pine wood is available, and it will not weather well. It is not clear how I will begin again to work my craft to support us, but begin I shall. Be patient, children, and hope."

Mama nods and takes his hand. Amelia and Paul answer that, yes, they will be patient and hope. I simply nod.

"Enough. We will give thanks and break bread," he says.

And we do, except that we have no bread. Mama has been feeding us potatoes, carrots, and onions from the root cellar. She boils them over an open fire in the hearth of what used to be the kitchen house. Snowflakes sizzle as they hit the fire, but Paul keeps it going with as many twigs and fragments of dry wood as he can find. Mama had us hide away some of our food when the blue coats first came last spring, but she says now that we must save it for when we become really hungry, so for the present we will just eat vegetables. I am really hungry now, but Mama must know what we should do. When Gus asks for milk, though, even Mama weeps. We have no cow; we have no milk. Yet when Papa prays he gives thanks for soup and candlelight and one another. Mama says as long as we are together, it will be all right. I want to believe her.

*****

December 1864
(About a week later)
Franklin, Tennessee

We are still sleeping in the root cellar, and I have started up again in the middle of the night from a bad dream, the same bad dream I have had for weeks, the one I have not been able to talk about with anyone.

The boy with the drum lies on his back, his arms flung out and his fingers curled slightly as if he were asleep, but I know that he is not asleep. He is too still—a child is never so still. He is a little older than I am, about the age of my brother Paul. In the dream, I wonder for a moment whether he is Paul, but then I am sure he is not, and for an instant I am glad. But how can I be glad? His eyes are open, and they are a startling blue. I must look away. I cannot look away. His red hair curls around his brow, and his skin—so fair—is freckled from the sun. He is completely still, and perfect, like the dead robin I once found in the garden—like our babies as they lay on the dining table—too perfect and too beautiful not to be alive. Though he is not my brother, I am as sorry as if he were.

*****

December 24, 1864
(Another week later)
Franklin, Tennessee

For the past month, though icy snow and wind have kept us shivering even under our blankets at night, we have been so active during the day that we have kept from freezing. Papa finished patching the big holes during the first week, but the rest of the repair is taking a long time. Since the wounded and dead soldiers were taken away, Mama, Amelia, and Paul have been helping to fix things, too. My job now is to stay in the root cellar with baby Gus, and to keep him safe. This would be fun if he weren't always so hungry, and if I weren't. Mama says it is hunger that makes him cry so much, and hunger that makes me impatient with him. That helps me to be kinder to him even though I don't at all feel like it. If it is just my gnawing stomach tormenting me, and not really Gus, there is nothing I can do to stop it, and I can just try to forget about it.

Nearly every one of the chickens and hogs, not only ours but everyone's throughout the town and countryside, has been eaten by the Yankee soldiers who are still occupying our town, still threatening, still stealing what is not theirs. Although Mama hid away our winter store of flour, the Yankees have torn down our kitchen house and so we had to wait for a break in the storm to repair the exposed oven and bake bread. Finally, yesterday Mama and Amelia were able to bake a few delicious-smelling loaves. Of course we wanted to eat them right away, but we are saving them for Christmas. Some neighbors in town have gotten new cows and have brought us milk and butter from time to time, so we have had a little something nice to add to our boiled vegetables from the root cellar.

"What is Christmas going to be like without any presents?" I ask Paul.

"What is it going to be like without food—real food, not just vegetable soup?"

We are in what once was the dining room, stuffing fresh paper in the gaps between the new boards and we think that no one hears us. We are mistaken.

"What is Christmas going to be like if we do not start thinking about someone other than ourselves?" Mama's voice replies from the hallway.

"Mama," Paul says, "your soup is as good as it can be seeing that it is only vegetables. Thank you for making bread."

Another mother might have laughed, but not Mama.

"It is not soup or bread that concerns me, son. Are we the only ones in this town who have suffered?"

"No, Mama," Paul answers, looking at the floor.

Mama is silent for a long moment before she asks, "How would you and Tillie like to play a game?"

We stare at her astonished, he answering an enthusiastic yes, I nodding. There have been no games these past weeks.

"For the next fifteen minutes, I want you to go upstairs and find all the food you can. I have hidden secret supplies in some very unlikely places, so you will need to use your thinking. You may look anywhere—in the closets, the bedrooms, any of the furniture. Put all the food you find in a basket—here, take this one—and carry it very carefully back down the ladder to me. I will wait here and tell you when your time is up."

Paul takes the basket and, laughing, climbs with me toward our mission, up and up the rough, wide ladder Papa has built between the first and second floors. We check the linen closet first, and surely enough, we find a jar of pickled tomatoes behind a pile of towels. Next, I look through the drawers in Mama's and Papa's room, something I have never been allowed to do before, and discover not one but two jars of jam, one blackberry and one currant. I wrap them in a towel, so they will not break against the jar of tomatoes, and lay them carefully in the basket. Paul emerges from his former bedroom with a long string of sausages around his neck.

"Can you guess where I found these?"

I shrug my shoulders and widen my eyes. I am getting good at talking with gestures.

"Under my mattress, of course. But we need mustard, you may be thinking."

I nod. That is exactly what I was thinking.

Paul pulls a jar from his pocket and waves it in the air. "It was in the pitcher on the wash stand!"

"Time is up," calls Mama from below.

Breathlessly, we scramble back down the ladder and lay our booty at her feet.

"Now we can have some tasty treats at Christmas, yes, Mama?"

She looks at Paul a long moment, and then says, "Are we the only ones who have suffered, son?"

Paul sighs, whether because he knows he is losing food or because he is disappointed in himself for forgetting so soon his earlier lesson, I cannot tell.

"No, Mama. But will we give it all away?"

"We will see what is needed to fill the basket nicely, and then we will see what is left."

We follow Mama to the kitchen where she empties the basket's contents onto the table and lines it with the towel. Then she begins to fill it again, first with large items—one of the loaves of bread we have been eyeing since yesterday and a bottle of elderberry cordial she has magically produced from someplace unknown. Next, she puts in a jar of jam—the blackberry, my favorite—and the jar of tomatoes, and some dried apples. Finally, when it is nearly overflowing, she takes the string of sausages from Paul's neck and with a sharp knife divides it in half, arranging one half among the other treats. I look at Paul, and he produces the mustard jar from his pocket and tucks it into a small space remaining.

"Can you lift this basket easily, Paul?" Mama asks, tying a red ribbon on the handle.

Paul lifts it and nods.

"Tillie, you go with him to open the doors. Go to the Carters' house now, and wish Mr. and Mrs. Carter a very merry Christmas from all our family. Give them this food with all your hearts, and remember that no one in our family has died in the battle."

*****

December 24, 1913 (Forty-nine years later)

Paris

Ferenc and I are celebrating our first Christmas as husband and wife. We have just returned from Mass at the cathedral where we were married just a few months ago. I am beginning to feel more comfortable praying here as I recognize more similarities to the Presbyterian services of my childhood and begin to appreciate the more sacramental Catholic Mass. This is a night to be hopeful, I thought as we walked home through beautiful Montmartre watching snow drift softly down.

Now our apartment glows with firelight and candles. Though it is deep winter, Ferenc has made sure that hothouse flowers bloom on our table—red roses, of course, and white chrysanthemums. Our cook has laid a feast of salmon *en croute*, caper cream sauce, blackberry *tarte*, and champagne.

Indeed, we have so much—everything this world can offer—our work, great success, whatever money can buy. But as we stand before the fire and Ferenc takes my hand, it is not any of those things that move me to silent thanksgiving. For the first Christmas in so many years, I have with me someone to care for, to share with. To take me out of my own small self and into who we are together, as Mama and Papa, Joseph, Amelia, Paul, Gus, and I were not separate but an entity together. This entity in which each of us is distinct but united is the finest gift this Christmas.

I have prepared Ferenc a basket of new oil paints, selecting each color carefully with an eye to his landscapes—phthalo blue and phthalo green, cadmium red, burnt umber—and a variety of new brushes, the best available. We have discovered a farm not far outside of the city, with a stone cottage and shapely barn that please Ferenc's eye, and a pasture of sheep that beckons me. Early tomorrow we will go out with our easels and palettes to catch the morning light.

*****

December 24, 1915 (Two years later)

Paris

How can I tell Ferenc that his constant chivalrous attentions are wearing on me, sometimes angering me? He is never cross, never self-absorbed as I so often am. When I speak sharply to him, he is silent. If I offend him, I never hear about it. His aim is always to give to me, to uphold me. I wish desperately that he would think more about himself, or at least stand back to allow me to think about myself. I wish he would rise in the morning and check with himself, rather than with me, about his goals for the day. I wish he would say no to me more often. I am probably a terrible wife, a terrible woman.

Is it true that in a marriage one person always loves more than the other? Or is it something other than love or lack of it that is the issue?

Ferenc is seldom anywhere but at my side. When we first became friends, I found his attentions charming, but in those days, after a pleasant interlude together, I would go off to Cairo or London, and he to Morocco or Vienna, and we would not see one another for a year or more. Reunions in Tata or Paris were usually brief since we both needed—and I, at least wanted—to pursue our separate work and lives.

When we were first married, I was concerned at the amount of time he wanted to spend together, but I told myself that we were newlyweds, and that his doting on me would diminish in time as we both fell into the rhythms of our creative lives. It has not. Ferenc usually paints alone, of course, as I do, but when he is not working, he sees my interests as his interests, my concerns as his concerns, even my annoyances—except, indeed, for this one—as his annoyances. I have come to disdain myself as one whose every whim is his object, from a blanket or a cup of tea to a pair of extravagant ruby earrings. Recently, when the noise from a neighbor's soirée went on a little late and might, just might, have disturbed my sleep, he rose from bed, dressed, and paid the neighbor a visit. I watched from the window as our good neighbor, charmed as everyone is by Count Blaskovits, sent his guests home. Was I happy? I was not. Who am I to be so completely catered to?

It may be that I have lived on my own for too long. I crave hours of solitude not only when I am painting, but often when I am resting. I often like to walk through Montmartre alone with my thoughts, or to read or sketch for hours undisturbed. I like to sit on the terrace or at a window in the morning, sipping coffee and planning the day's activities. At night, I need to pray and contemplate alone, to remember who I am before the One I shall ultimately face alone. Ferenc would accompany me during any and all of these times if I did not steal some privacy. He is never reproachful, but when I insist on solitude he seems wistful, while I am distracted by self-reproach.

I think that, when young, most women must be very adaptable. They yield not only their hours and days, but their very bodies to their husbands and to their children. This is right and good. Sadly, disastrously, many yield their minds, as well. This is wrong; this is what I fear. But Ferenc would not wish such a thing.

Though I am neither young nor adaptable, though I cannot give away my mind and soul, I will give to our marriage what is right. Do I care for, admire, and desire my husband? I do. Do I continue to commit myself to our union? I do.

Yet romance and courtliness, as distinct from love and passion, often suffocate me so that I feel panic when we are together for a long time without respite. When I married, I did not become the lady fair of Count Ferenc Blaskovits, but rather his helpmate. Our relationship began in friendship, and friendship is wonderfully free. In friendship wed to passion it must continue.

As Papa once said about another situation, here I have several difficult truths existing together. I have to find a way for Ferenc to understand, though it may take a long while. I will begin tonight.

*****

DECEMBER 24, 1915
(THE EVENING OF THAT SAME DAY)

Paris, France

Ferenc and I have spent Christmas Eve at the basilica and later shared food and wine, holding hands as we sat beside the fire. Now we are lying in bed in each other's arms.

"Tillie, we should go to the country tomorrow morning as we did on our first Christmas. We can sketch in the dawn light, and eat our breakfast under blankets in the carriage."

"We had a wonderful day that first Christmas in the country. But—"

"Do you remember the bird? La Perdrit Rouge?"

"Yes, the partridge with the red legs and beak. He perched on the snow-covered fence, fluttering his white and black feathers. I sketched him."

"And on the way home you taught me to sing 'The Partridge in a Pear Tree' and we made our own verses."

"On the first day of Christmas, my true love gave to me, one happy marriage and a partridge in a pear tree."

"On the second day of Christmas, my true love gave to me, two hands to hold and a partridge in a pear tree."

"Ferenc, I do want to go to the country with you tomorrow morning."

"Good."

"And I want to spend the afternoon alone."

"Yes?"

"Yes, Ferenc, I want to walk. Alone. I need to do that."

I feel his head nodding silently, and he pulls me closer.

"And I want to dine with you in the evening, and to sing Christmas carols, and to hold you like this."

We have no more need for words this Christmas Eve. This is a good beginning.

*****

DECEMBER 25, 1864 (FORTY-ONE YEARS EARLIER, THE CHRISTMAS AFTER THE BATTLE)

Franklin, Tennessee

In spite of all that has happened, Christmas really has come. For the past month while my voice has been silent, the inside of me has been loud like the battle, with thoughts and feelings fighting each other. Today my inside has been still, like the land itself is still under the snow. Papa says that the kind, white snow is covering the wounded land until it begins to heal.

After the church service this morning, people gathered around us to fill Mama's and Papa's arms with bundles, saying that we and the Carters have suffered the worst of all. When we got home and opened their packages, we could hardly believe our eyes—milk, butter, bread, blackberry pies, a bottle of wine, and a big piece of ham that we all said was the most delicious we had ever eaten. Mama said that hunger is the best sauce and we have brought plenty of that to our feast today.

Since we have our new coal-burning fireplace,. we have been able to eat dinner at our dining table, now moved to the parlor.

Mama and Amelia have covered it with a lace cloth and set it with our finest dishes. We are dressed in our finest, as well—Mama in a dark-red wool gown with her cameo brooch at the throat, Amelia in green muslin, and I in my best blue dress with the skirt that bells out when I twirl in a circle. I wonder whether Tod Carter can see me from wherever he is if he is somewhere still.

Though we have no piano, we sing carols after our feast. "*O Tannenbaum*" is Paul's favorite—"O Christmas Tree" in English, which is funny because we have no Christmas tree, nor do we have any trees at all, but only a vase of holly. The holly is pretty with its red berries, though, and Paul and I hung paper snowflakes from its branches. My favorite carol is "*Stille Nacht.*" They sang it in English at church today, "Silent night, holy night. All is calm, all is bright."

All is truly calm and bright tonight. I do not know how it can be, but it is.

Our family is gathered in front of the new fireplace. It is wonderful to be warm and full, resting here together. Even Joseph has come to stay with us for the feast, and will stay a while longer to help us continue to rebuild. In the quiet before bedtime, I am drawing again for the first time since the battle. I am completing my drawing of Mattie, so that I can remember her always. It surprises me how clearly I see her in memory, how natural it is to recreate her deep-brown eyes and the lines and curves of her young body, the laughing tilt of her head.

Mama looks up from the socks she is knitting and smiles at me. She is still my strong, stern Mama, but she has been very sweet to me in these past weeks, speaking to me often and gently, stroking my hair, reassuring me that I will be able to talk again when I am ready, when my heart and body have had time to heal. Many years later, while I am painting in Mama's native Bavaria, I will taste the delicious *eiswein*, a special wine made from grapes left long on the vine until the frost draws into them the sweet sap that is deep inside the wood. No other wine is as rich or as sweet as the one pressed from frostbitten, weather-beaten grapes. Perhaps this desperate winter, Mama's sweetness has been perfected like the *eiswein.*

*****

January 1865 (The next month)

Franklin, Tennessee

I look at Papa in confusion. I have not been able to speak since the battle, though I have tried as hard as I ever could. I have thought of words and I have opened my mouth, but no words have come. Papa knows this, yet still he is waiting for me to speak—to speak this very moment. He does not break his gaze, but keeps looking at me and nodding. He puts his hand on my shoulder and waits.

I did not suspect anything when Papa built a shed in the yard this week with some wood left over from fixing the house. It was strange to see him working out in the icy cold, but when I asked what he was doing, he told me that I would soon see. Then this morning he went off to work in town, and he when he returned he told me to put on my coat and boots, and led me to the backyard.

There beside the porch was a beautiful cow, not black and white like Ute and Mattie, but a delicious brown, like chocolate. I laughed out loud for the first time since the battle. I laughed and cried and laughed again. Maybe this is what made Papa hope that I would speak now.

"She is a brown Swiss heifer, Tillie," Papa said.

I ran to her and threw my arms around her silky, warm neck.

But then Papa said, "You shall name her."

And now here I stand, my words frozen, his hand on my shoulder.

"Go ahead, my Tillie. Tell me, what is her name?"

Her coat is like the lovely brown hair of a girl named Bertha who sings in the church choir, but Mama doesn't want us to name an animal exactly after a person. Maybe we could call her Bertie, though, like Mattie instead of Matilda. I put my lips together, and push out the air as hard as hard as I can.

"Be…"

Papa stands steady, not saying a word or showing any emotion, simply waiting and believing.

"Bert…" I whisper.

Papa nods.

"Bert!" I say with all my might.

Papa lifts me into the air. "Hallelujah! Bert she shall be, my Matilda!"

The whole family calls our new calf Bert, but after I am more practiced at speaking again, I call her Bertie.

*****

April 16, 1865 (Three months later)

Franklin, Tennessee

It is Easter day, and the sun is bright in the still, chilly air. As we walk home from church, Mama says the snow will be melted from the graves of the soldiers, and we should visit them. I do not want to visit the graves of soldiers. I do not ever want to see a soldier or think about a soldier again, but Mama would be sad if I said so.

No wildflowers grow on those new mounds of earth, but grass has begun to sprout on some—young and brightly gold-green.

"Mama, where is the boy?" I ask, suddenly remembering.

"Which boy, Tillie?"

"The boy who was little like me. In a blue uniform. He had a drum."

Mama stoops down from her height to take my face in her gloved hands. Her cheeks are pink with the cold air; her eyes, meeting mine, are wet.

"Matilda, dear, did you see that little drummer boy lying near our house when we returned after the battle?"

I nod, dissolving into tears. "I am so sorry, Mama. I was trying to look up, but we were almost home and I wanted to see our house, but then there was a drum in the road and he was just lying there…"

Mama kneels down right there, on the wet and muddy grass, in her best black silk dress. She takes me into her great, safe embrace. We do not speak. She has tried to protect me from this suffering, and I have tried to obey her, but we have both failed. We are sorry for each other's pain and for our own, and for the little boy with the drum. After a long time, when I stop sobbing, she leans back to look at me.

"I do not know where they have laid him, Tillie. He was with the Northern army, and their soldiers came to take him away from our yard. They buried many of their soldiers right here in Franklin, but there are almost no markers, so there is no telling one grave from the other. Likely his body lies nearby. But he is not in his body anymore, Tillie. I have no doubt that he is with the Lord who loves him."

"But he was with the blue uniforms that killed Tod."

"He was with the Northern army, but it is a person's heart that matters, not his circumstances. We did not know him, but it appears that what he did was to play the drum for people he knew and trusted. He did not kill anybody. Do you understand?"

I shake my head. "No. I do not understand. Where is he, Mama? Where is Tod Carter? Where is Mattie?"

Mama smiles—not a happy smile, but a serene one. "It's all right, Tillie. There is time for you to understand this. For now, let us commend the little boy to his Lord, and say good-bye to him."

We bow our heads as Mama prays that God will keep the little drummer boy with Him in His joy. The faint, early spring sun warms the backs of our necks and our raised hands. When we finish, Mama takes my hand and holds it all the way home.

After that day, though I remember him often, I do not dream again of the drummer boy.

*****

NOVEMBER 16, 1898 (THIRTY-THREE YEARS LATER)

Paris

My heart freezes at the knock. I summon my will, forcing my feet to carry me to the door. It is as I have feared—the telegram from Papa. I must grip the door frame to steady myself, and somehow, I cannot remember how, I manage to pay the deliveryman and close the door behind him.

The envelope is pink and tissue-like. It does not seem substantial enough to carry the weight of this news. My hands tremble so that I have difficulty opening it and finally rip it in two. Inside is more flimsy pink paper.

1898 NOV 16 PM 3 57

Johann Albert Lotz.
San Francisco California USA

My Tillie, your dear mama is gone peacefully,
little pain. Will write very soon. Your papa.

I sit for a long while looking out the window at the cold rain, the bare trees swaying. I am swaying in the wind of this loss.

Papa's last letter arriving two weeks ago detailed Mama's decline. I know that he wrote immediately when she began to fail, to give me time to prepare. But can one actually prepare? There is a piercing emptiness in my chest as if an organ has been pulled from it, a lung perhaps, since it is difficult to breathe.

I tell myself that it was inevitable, that she has had seventy-eight years rich in love and creativity, that we have been blessed to have her so long. All this is true. But what of dear, ethereal Papa? How will he cope without her steady strength?

If only our last visit had been better. We had been separated for so long, and I was not the girl who had left home for Paris six years before. She thought she knew me, but she did not, and I could not stay long enough for a new understanding to grow. Words can go only so far. Maybe now she knows what she has always meant to me.

*****

October 1887
(Eleven years earlier)

San Jose, California

"I cannot understand why New York will be better for you than San Francisco," Mama says yet again.

We are saying our good-byes at my parents' home before my imminent move. Nervously, I trace with my forefinger the imprint of a cluster of cherries that Papa has carved into the arm of the chair. I used to love to close my eyes and run my fingers over all the carvings of the furniture he made for us—the chairs and tables, and especially the piano decorated with roses and apples. Now I feel restless and confined in this parlor—there is too much furniture, or else the furniture, for all its beauty, is too big for the room. The air is close and I am having difficulty breathing.

"San Francisco is a newer city, Mama," I explain again, trying to sound calm. "Certainly it has people who value art, but evidently it does not have enough for me to make a living."

"What about Mr. Dan Cook, who was so generous when you were at the School of Design? Have you approached him?"

"That was twelve years ago, Mama. I do not even know where he is."

"You still have the Hearsts, though, and the Stanfords. They believe in you."

"They have always been wonderful, Mama, but you know that they cannot support me, nor would I ask them to. I need to work, and they need only so many paintings."

"Oh, I don't know," Paul chimes in, grinning. "Their houses are pretty big. They might keep you busy for a few years at least, covering all those walls."

Dear Paul, always able to make me laugh, to lighten a difficult situation. It has been wonderful sharing a house with him this past year, and especially sharing a studio, where we have worked side by side as we did when we were children. I normally cannot bear to have anyone near me when I am painting, but Paul is an exception. It is through his thoughtful glances over my shoulder and his respectful critique that I have learned to draw and paint in the first place. Now he is a very successful photographer, in partnership with T. H. Jones at the Elite Photography Studio on Market Street. We are both working at our art as we always dreamed of doing. Paul has said he is as sad as any of us that I must leave now, but leave I must, and he accepts it.

"How do you know that you will be able to make a living in New York?" Mama continues.

"I don't. But as long as I am back in the United States, I may as well try, and at least study and exhibit for a while, even if I do not receive commissions or sell any paintings."

"But you could live here with us, Tillie, couldn't she, Albert?"

"Tillie always has a home with us, Margaretha, but she is a woman now, a professional painter, with a life of her own."

I smile gratefully at my dear papa who has always understood me. He looks tired these days, fading gradually and sweetly like the light at the end of the day.

"Amelia did not mind living here as a grown woman. She was thirty-five when she married, six years older than you are now,

Matilda. You are such a lovely girl, and so intelligent. Surely many eligible young men would be interested in you. What about the gentleman who called shortly after you returned last November?"

I look at Paul and roll my eyes. I will not lose my patience. Paul's presence will help me.

"Do you mean the gentleman who once attended the School of Design with me, Mama? The one who came to tea?

"Yes. What was his name? Mr. Schmitt, Mr. Schutz?"

"Mr. Herbert Schneider. What of him, Mama?"

"It seemed he wished to keep company with you."

"Yes."

"Do you not like him?"

I take a deep breath and release it slowly before I speak. As Mama sees it, we should all remain together, and she is marshalling all her strength to keep me from leaving. What is art compared with the family? It is useless to try to explain. I smile at her and remember how much I love her, how much I respect her, in spite of the battle she is waging today.

"I like him, Mama. He is a talented and interesting associate, and I believe he will do well locally with family portraiture. But if you are asking whether I am interested in keeping company with him, the answer is no, I am not interested in keeping company with him or with any man. I want to paint professionally and well, and to be free to go wherever I can do that."

Mama is looking at me steadily, and it seems there are tears in her eyes, though it may be the way the light is falling on her face, the strong, determined face of one who has suffered for me, fought for me, shown me how to be strong. It is difficult for her, now that I am strong. I rise from the chair and go to her, leaning my head on hers and circling her shoulder with my arm. It will be easier to say what I must say if I do not need to look into her eyes, if we are not facing each other poised for argument.

"Mama, I am so grateful for everything you and Papa have

done for me, and for who you are. Just the thought of you both has strengthened me the whole time I was struggling to establish myself in Paris, and I know it will always be that way.

"If I could become a great painter in San Francisco, I would like so much to visit you every week and to share life with you as we used to do. That is why I came here, with the seed of that hope. It has not come to fruition, Mama. I have had scarcely any work here in more than a year. I have to go now. I am taking you with me in my heart."

Mama is indeed weeping now, and so am I. She stands to embrace me, and I kiss her firm, soft cheek as I loved to do as a child. Then Papa brings around the carriage to drive Paul and me back to San Francisco. I will leave for New York in the morning. We do not speak again in person, not ever again in this life.

*****

May 1865
(Twenty-two years earlier)

Franklin, Tennessee

The snow and ice have finally melted in the gentle sunshine, and the grass is growing quickly, turning our yard green and covering the sad tree stumps that reminded us of so much we have lost.

Bertie grazes in the pasture and Paul teaches me how to draw her big, gentle head bowed to graze on the tender new shoots. Paul is skilled and patient as he puts his hand over mine to guide the pencil strokes.

"The shading is darker here, and there is a more curved line here, like this… Isn't that the way you see her?"

He sees very much as I see, and because he has been practicing for several years longer, he is better at making what we see visible on the paper. But he listens closely to my comments if I disagree with him. These early drawings are not mine, not his, but ours. Paul has helped me to finish my drawing of Mattie, too, from the vivid images we still have in our minds' eye. Soon I will learn to paint her, and my painting will help keep her in our memories.

But we are looking now at today's beauty more than yesterday's, as Amelia often says this spring. On a warm morning when the wildflowers have begun to bloom, Amelia packs a picnic and takes Paul, Gus, and me to climb the hills to see them. It is wonderful to walk, and especially to climb, after so many months of confinement in the snow and cold. The air is cool and the ground is muddy with melting snow, so we still wear our winter coats and boots, but the sun is warm on our faces and shoulders. The wet air smells of mud and grass as we pause to catch our breath.

When we reach the first meadow, we find white evening primrose, nearly as tall as I am, with long stems lifting the four heart-shaped petals to my eyes. Then stooping to the ground, we find the sweet, nectar-fragranced red clover, bees buzzing around its pink pips with golden-brown tips. Sometimes this clover used to spring up in our pasture, but it didn't last long with hungry Ute and Mattie and the hungry sheep. Here it covers most of the meadow, untouched.

As we climb higher, we find the mountain laurel—clusters of small, white umbrellas dotted inside with crimson and trimmed with green. But my very favorite is the maypop—a pale lady just like a doll, with arms held out as if in a dance and an extravagant fringed skirt of purple and white. We gather a few of each flower to bring to Mama, who spends most of these spring days sewing linens to replace those we used to bind the wounds of the soldiers.

The war has ended, and the Northern army has won. Some blue soldiers stay in the town and tell people what to do, and Mama and Papa do not like it, but they say they are thankful that there will be no more battles. Mama says she is sorry about the Yankee soldiers who got blown up by accident on the big ship with the long name that starts with an "L," when they were on their way home to their families. She says that, Yankees or not, they are people's sons and husbands, and it is sad that they had to die.

I don't know how, with all the sorrow they have brought us, she is able to find more sorrow for their deaths. If they had died earlier, they might never have come here.

*****

November 29, 1865
(Six months later)

Franklin, Tennessee

Mama enters the darkened room bearing the surprise she has been promising—an amazing cake, layers high, decorated with red berries and seven candles. The candlelight captures the love in her eyes as she looks at me, the pride of accomplishment in the set of her wide, firm mouth. Since our fruit trees and nut trees are all gone, Mama has gathered the apples and pecans for this cake from neighbors in town, trading with our milk and eggs. And now we have Bertie's sweet, creamy milk ourselves, to go with the cake. Our dining room is patched and dark, but Mama has laid the table with our good china and silver to make a seventh birthday party for me, and I have put on my best blue cotton dress with white lace and white pantaloons. It is tighter and shorter than it was last year, but still my favorite.

Earlier this evening, after dinner and before the cake, Papa was teaching me how to waltz, and the skirts of my dress spun out like the petals of a flower. First I stood on Papa's feet and felt the way he was moving as he twirled me around the room. Then I stood on my own and followed as he led me, first in slow, small circles, and then in wide, sweeping ones. It was the loveliest feeling to glide with Papa to the movement of the music. After a while I did not even think of where my feet would go, but moved as I think a bird must fly—naturally, joyfully.

Now the best part of the evening has come—the cake and the song.

"Amelia, will you lead?" Mama asks.

Everyone in our family likes to sing, but Amelia is the true musician, the one who is always asked to sing solos in the church choir, and for whom Papa, as soon as he could make the house livable again, has repaired our family piano. Now she makes a little extra money for us by giving piano lessons, but she also brightens our evenings by playing. She begins to sing in her high, precise soprano voice. Papa joins in, his voice warm and light as a summer sky. I later learn that his voice is called tenor, and that Mama's rich, deep tones are called alto. Paul sings, too, and even Gus, lisping. They sing for me a traditional German birthday song:

Viel Gluck und viel Segen
Auf all Deinen Wegen,
Gesundheit und Fohsinn
Sei auch mit dabei!

It means much luck and many blessings on all your ways, good health and cheerfulness be also with you. I look around the table at each of them—Papa's gentle, sensitive face, Mama's often stern face smiling widely at my happiness, Paul's and Gus's excitement as they eye the cake and fruit—and I tell myself to remember this moment forever. Then I blow out the seven candles, taking an extra breath for the last one, the candle of this last, most difficult year. I am thankful that it is my last birthday party we are remembering together, and not those other days immediately following, though the consequences of the battle will return to plague us for longer than we had imagined.

*****

July 1869

(Four years later)

Franklin, Tennessee

A loud pounding on the front door freezes my hand in mid-sketch. Paul and I look at each other fearfully. The pounding continues, forceful, not the tap of a neighborly visit. Papa answers, and Paul and I hide around the corner in the parlor to listen. From the parlor window we see two men on our porch and four others who are holding horses in the street at the foot of the walkway.

"Albert Lotz?" barks a tall man with a bristly red beard and a face like a pig's—little, deep-set dark eyes set in rolls of reddened flesh.

"Yes, I am Johann Albert Lotz," Papa answers in his formal, mild way.

"We hear you've been making a pianny."

"Indeed, more than one. I am a woodworker."

"Y-e-s-s-s, but this one is partic-a-lar," drawls the pig man.

"Oh, how so?" answers Papa.

Something is wrong; this is not a friendly visit. If it were, Papa would have asked these people to come in and sit down. Instead, he steps out of the house and closes the door behind him. I help Paul to lift the window nearest the porch as quietly as we can, to listen.

"We hear that this par-tic-a-lar pianny got an American eagle on it, is that right?"

"Sir, I am not sure I like your tone. Would you kindly identify yourself, and introduce these people with you?"

"Well, pretty much all you need to know is that we here are members of the Klan over to Pulaski, couple counties south of here, and we've come to take a look at your pianny."

For the past year, Papa has been working in most of his spare time on a wonderful new piano. He has used the best rosewood he could obtain, and crafted each part with all his skills. Now that the war has been over for several years, Papa wants to make this piano as a memorial to peace in the nation, so he has carved on top of the front panel a great American eagle with outstretched wings, holding the Federal flag and the Confederate flag, one in each talon. I think it is one of the loveliest pieces he has ever made.

Papa hesitates and then says, "Well, I do not see any harm in your looking at the piano. It is out in my workshop, behind the house. But I will ask that only one or two of you come with me, so we do not alarm my family."

Papa's words bring me back to that other day when many frightening men were at our door. I catch my breath, and Paul puts his arm around my shoulder.

The pig man nods at the man next to him, also tall but thin, with a leathery face, and wearing a Confederate uniform even though the Confederacy lost the war years ago. These must be the two leaders of this group. They follow Papa down the stairs and around to the back of the house, while the others—five of them—stand out front with the horses. Paul and I tear off down the hall to the kitchen and out the back door, where we can hide around the corner of the house near enough to Papa's workshop to hear their voices.

It is not difficult to hear the voices of the visitors who soon are shouting.

"See there, Glover," says the leathery uniformed man. "It's just as we hear'd. That eagle is desecratin' the Confederate flag!"

"It surely seems to be so, Seth," the pig man drawls menacingly.

"Gentlemen, you misunderstand! This is meant as a monument to peace now that the war is over. It is meant to respect both North and South, to bring the two together."

"The two will never be together, German, though I doubt you could understand that since you don't belong here."

The last snarling remark is in the voice of the leathery man. How could someone speak to Papa so?

But Papa does not answer angrily. He merely says, "Sir, I have lived, worshipped, and worked in this community for many years. It is my home, and no one regrets the bloody war more deeply than I."

"Mmph," snorts the leathery voice.

"Be that as it *might*," pig man answers, "there is no denying that this eagle's claw is digging into the flag of our Confederacy just like it was a rabbit to devour. Can you deny that, Lotz?"

"I do not deny that the talon grips the flag, but this is how the grain of the wood demands I carve it. I do deny your interpretation. The eagle is holding both flags together, lifting both together—"

"Say what you want, German, this is an insult that will not go unpunished!" leather man shouts.

"We are the power now. It's up to us to keep the Confederacy alive, Lotz, and you have not cooperated," pig man threatens.

They emerge from the workshop, the two angry men pushing Papa backward toward the house. My heart is beating nearly out of my chest. Paul, who is now twelve, is about to go to Papa to help him when Papa raises his open palm in the air to speak.

"Gentlemen, I have no quarrel with you, and certainly none with the Confederacy."

"Your actions speak more loudly, German," says leather man, moving toward the front of the house.

Papa stands on the porch as they ride away, his dear hands hanging helplessly by his sides. Suddenly, he looks older than ever he has before.

*****

Late July 1869 (About two weeks later)

Franklin, Tennessee

Mama is crying. Papa is continuing to question his friend from Giles County who has arrived breathless a short time before. Paul and I are not supposed to be listening, but of course we are listening from our perch on the stairs that allows us to hear everything, even through closed doors. We have sent Gus out to the kitchen to "help" Amelia just in case something frightening is going on.

Something frightening is going on.

"Yes, I am certain of what I have heard. It is rumored everywhere. The Ku Klux Klan wants to tar and feather you, right here in your own yard. They want to make an example of you."

"Because of a piano?"

"Because of many things, Albert. This is difficult to say but you must understand. Many people in Tennessee call you a neighbor and a friend, but you are not from here. You and your son did not fight for us."

Papa nods slowly. "Yes, I see. So they would kill me?"

Mama lets out a sob.

"Worse, Albert. They would cover your body with liquid tar

that would strip the skin right off of you. Then they would pour feathers over you to mock you, which might just smother you to death. If you survived, and I say *if*, you would be hideously disfigured for the rest of your life, and a laughingstock among those who do not know you for the man you are. Your reputation would be destroyed. There is nothing to do but flee."

"But my family would have to leave everything they know and love. And my business—I have just begun to turn a real profit again. And the house I have built, and rebuilt, with my own hands.

"I know, Albert. I would like to see you and your family stay in your home and continue to contribute to this community, but to stay would almost surely cost you your life, and perhaps endanger your family, as well."

"We must go, Albert," Mama says, wiping her tears and speaking with a firmness that gives me courage. "There is no question. We must go as soon as ever we can."

"Your wife is a wise woman, Albert. Do not think twice about this." The visitor stands to leave. "And do not speak my name to anyone in connection with this if you have ever been my friend."

"Of course, of course. I am deeply grateful to you for your kindness, William. No doubt I owe you my life."

When the adults begin to say their good-byes, we quickly steal upstairs to the hallway, looking at each other in fear and disbelief. The worst part is not being able to ask Papa and Mama what it all means. I cry, and Paul puts his arm around my shoulder. I can feel his body trembling. Then he is crying, too.

*****

August 1869
(Two days later)

Franklin, TN

Mama gathers Amelia, Paul, Gus, and me into the library where Papa is sitting in his reading chair. It is early evening, just before dinner, and a gentle light filters through the window and onto his face. The feeling of the room is as quiet and serious as if we were in church. We stand before him, and Mama takes her place behind him, her hand on his shoulder. Papa's explanation is simple and irrefutable.

"My dear children, we have a situation that demands that we leave our home," he begins.

Amelia catches her breath, her hand flying to her mouth, the color draining from her face. She grips a side table for support. Paul and I look at each other, trying to show surprise, hoping that Papa and Mama will not guess that we already know. Gus, who is only seven, truly is surprised, his mouth opening and shutting soundlessly like a puppet's.

"Your mother and I have had to move many times before," he continues. "We know how to prepare for our journey, and in fact we have already begun to prepare. There is nothing to be concerned about."

"But where will we go, Papa?" Gus blurts out.

"In a moment, Augustus," Mama says.

"The great difficulty, of course, will be leaving this house, which has been a fine home to us, and leaving the Carters and other neighbors who are true friends," Papa continues. "But as I have said, your mother and I have done this before. We know that we can build a new home, and that we will find kind and good people anywhere we go."

Amelia is nodding, so Paul and I nod, too, but Mama is searching our faces. She knows us well; surely she guesses from our lack of emotion that we are not hearing about this for the first time. Her brow is wrinkling.

"Augustus, you would like to know where we are going, and I will tell you. We shall cross the country to the State of California," Papa says.

Now it is Paul who gasps, but with enthusiasm—this truly is news, and a great adventure. My heart is beating quickly, and I do not know whether I am terrified or excited, or perhaps both. I take Paul's hand and squeeze it tightly.

"There is a great deal of opportunity in California, and many people are choosing to relocate there, so we will not only have companions for our journey, but customers for the woodworking business when we arrive." Papa pauses, and looks up at Mama. "You need to understand, children, that we must act very quickly to leave the town of Franklin within the next two weeks."

My stomach lurches. Paul takes his hand away to rub it, and I realize that I have been digging my fingernails into his palm. Now, added to the threats made to Papa, are the fear of swift change, and the fear of the unknown.

Neither Mama nor Papa speaks for a moment, so Paul does. "Papa, what will be our route? Will we go through Indian country?

Will we drive a covered wagon? Will we join a wagon train? Will we take the animals? Will we take our belongings with us?"

Papa gives a little laugh and holds up his hand. "One question at a time, son. We have been advised not to attempt the Oregon-California Trail this year, since it is already August, and we could not hope to arrive at Independence, Missouri, to embark for at least another month. This would risk impassable winter weather, especially in the western mountains. Your mama has written to her cousin in Germantown outside of Memphis, and we have been invited to stay with her family until early spring of next year when we will head north to Independence to begin the Trail. Amelia, you met Cousin Hilda and her husband Rudi, ahem, Herr Schotter, while we were living in Nashville. Do you remember them?"

Amelia clears her throat. "Yes, I remember them. It is very kind of them to ask us to stay." Amelia does not seem enthusiastic about the reunion. She still looks white as milk, and her eyes are shining as if she is about to cry, though she does not.

"Indeed it is kind of them to put up an entire family for so many months," says Mama. "We will do all we can to be a help to them, and not a burden."

All of us children nod or murmur agreement.

"Now, Paul, you would like to know what we will take with us," Papa continues. "The answer is that we will take very little, only what will fit into about one half of a wagon, since the other half will be filled with provisions. We will be living very simply for a while." He looks at Amelia and smiles so tenderly that she returns his smile, though hers trembles. It will be very hard for Amelia to leave her piano, her lessons, and her students, not to mention her friends and possible beaus. For Paul, Gus, and me, our home itself is largely our world, but Amelia has been discovering a larger world, and will have to put it aside for a time.

"Now, I think it is time for supper," Mama says briskly. "Chicken and dumplings in honor of our new beginnings." She doesn't need to tell us, since the delicious aroma fills the house. I guess we will not need the chickens for much longer.

Papa rises and walks toward the dining room. He has not answered Paul's question about the Indians, but I am sure Paul will keep asking until he finds out.

*****

LATE AUGUST 1869 (TWO WEEKS LATER)

Franklin, Tennessee

Change has swept in on us like a mighty storm, lifting our family in its updraft and ultimately carrying us away, will we, nil we. We surrender to its currents because we must.

During these last weeks in our home, I study Papa's and Mama's faces from day to day. I want to learn how they are dealing with this crisis, to understand how to carry the confusion of feelings in my heart. Neither of them ever seems to change, neither ever wavers, at least not in the sight of us children. They speak very little—practical details about our tasks or words of encouragement, but they seem to say with each look and movement: *This is the burden we have been given; we will simply carry it, and we will help one another to carry it.* This is what I try to do, though I cannot stop thinking about the pig man and the leather man and the mean-looking men they brought with them—another army, more horrible people who are trying to hurt us when we weren't hurting anybody. It is so unfair that it makes my stomach hurt.

Strangers come and go as Papa sells our dining table and the chairs where we sat to take our meals together, our sofas and soft chairs where we sat to read and talk, his desk and bookshelves, even most of his treasured books. He sells the fine wood for making furniture that he has accumulated with such difficulty since the battle. And then, unimaginably, he sells our house.

One morning during those whirlwind weeks, Paul and I are in the west pasture sketching the sheep with a new urgency, since soon they, too, will be gone. The light is wonderful, shining with early morning clarity on their faces, casting cool shadows onto the tall, dewy grass. Paul and I sit side by side on the split-rail fence, the sun warming our backs, the air still cool enough to allow us to concentrate, as it will not be by late morning.

As I have gotten older and practiced drawing and painting faithfully, Paul has become less a teacher, and more a supportive companion. He is fifteen now, slim and strong, and the gold of his hair has darkened to warm brown hues. The older he becomes, the more he is like Papa in appearance, though his nature is more adventurous. Everyone says that I am taking after Mama, which makes me proud.

After that visit when Papa's friend brought the terrible news about the people with the strange clan name threatening us, I have never seen Mama cry, even though the world of her home is vanishing piece by piece around her. Instead, she seems to stand even taller than usual, to set her mouth yet more firmly. She moves from task to task as she once moved from one wounded soldier to the next while making no distinction between blue-clad or gray, simply performing any service necessary to the dreadful emergency.

Today, as Paul and I draw, Mama is packing up her china and crystal from Bavaria to give to Cousin Hilda, saying that it will not survive a trip across the country in a wagon, and that it is better to make space for food than for fancy dishes. Yet yesterday she helped me to wrap up my china doll Greta, and to put her to sleep safely in our trunk of clothes.

I am erasing my last few pencil strokes and trying again to capture the shadows in the curls of the sheep's coat, when a rider arrives in front of our house. Paul and I look at each other fearfully.

"Do you think it could be one of those clan people?" I ask Paul.

"I don't think so. Those men were in a group, the way bullies usually like to be. This man seems to be alone."

We jump down from the fence, and hurry toward the side of the house while the man ties his horse and walks up the front steps. I am relieved to see that he is not one of the men who was here before. When he knocks, it is politely. Papa comes to the door.

"Mr. Lotz?"

"Yes, Johann Albert Lotz. And you are Mr. Robert G. Buchanan, I believe?"

They shake hands. Paul and I breathe more easily as they disappear into the house and we run around to the back door and through the hallway. But they are still in the hallway, talking, and we quickly duck into the dining room to listen.

"Yes, I built the house myself in 1858. I am a master woodworker, and I put a lot of careful attention into the floors, the windows, the mantelpieces, and especially the staircase. But as I explained in detail in answer to your letter, the house suffered a great deal of damage during the 1865 battle, and between scarcity of materials and scarcity of time, I have not been able to make the repairs as well as I wanted."

"Yes, yes, of course. I fully understand, sir. We do not, any of us, live as we did before the war."

They stand a moment in profound silence.

"May I give you a tour of the house then?"

Papa leads Mr. Buchanan from room to room of our home, the home in which I have spent each day and night of my nearly eleven years. Papa displays the spaces of our shared life as he has displayed so many of our cherished belongings, calmly, matter-of-factly. Mr. Buchanan remarks often on the fine quality of

Papa's woodwork, murmurs dismissively when Papa apologizes for one or another of the hasty repairs. When they walk outside to view the rebuilt workshop, kitchen house, smokehouse, and barn, and the restored pastures, Paul and I watch from the back porch. Over the past five years since the battle, our new pecan, apple, and peach trees have thrived, and now give our grounds an appealing look. There is no doubt that Mr. Buchanan likes what he sees.

They return to the house and enter the library, out of our view. Paul and I take our perch on the stairway to catch what we can of their conversation.

"I am definitely interested in purchasing the property, Mr. Lotz. What is your asking price?"

"I am asking for one thousand dollars, Mr. Buchanan. My family and I will need that amount to relocate."

Mr. Buchanan whistles and chuckles. "It would take me until some time early next year to raise that amount. But if you would take $850, I can make the transaction by the end of November."

They are silent for a while. In my mind's eye, I can see Papa's sincere, intelligent face as he considers the balance between our need for haste and our need for money.

"I would accept $900, if you could complete the transaction by the end of November. I will be staying with relatives near Memphis and could meet you to finalize the transaction. And I will include the piano you liked so well."

Paul nudges my arm and we exchange a knowing look. Our Papa is a very clever businessman—that piano with the eagle gripping the flags is the spark that ignited all our trouble in the first place. Surely Papa is very glad to be rid of it, and the bullies will forget all about it once we are gone.

There is another moment of silence.

"Done," Mr. Buchanan says.

"Let's have a glass of cordial to seal our agreement," Papa offers. As they move across the room, we lose the rest of their conversation.

Papa tells us the news at supper.

"I had to make a great sacrifice, though," he says with a wry smile. "I have included the fancy carved piano in the sale."

"*Gott sei Dank!*" cries Mama. "Thanks be to God!" And we all laugh.

*****

September 1869 (Two weeks later)

Franklin, TN

We are seated in our wagon, surrounded by our few possessions. Though Mama and Papa have not spoken again of the urgency of our preparations to leave, I am sure that I am not the only one who is relieved that the pig man and the other clan bullies have not come back yet.

We have sacrificed most of what we owned, and now we will give up our home. Mama has been telling me, and I tell myself, that I am a big girl—ten years old, nearly eleven. I am with the ones I love. I can endure this thing.

Papa is taking a last survey of the property, making fast the locks, making sure that all is left in order for the new owner. His face is like the faces of the Old Testament prophets in our family Bible—Elijah or Isaiah—neither happy nor sad, but wonderfully steady. We wait for what is probably only a few moments, but what seems an hour, suspended between what our life has been and what it will become.

We are leaving times of fear and of suffering, yes, but, even recently, many times of sweetness. I memorize the lines of the stately white house, its pillars, its porches, its tall windows framed with black shutters. In memory, I see Amelia, her long, graceful neck bent over the piano. I see Mama in the kitchen, proudly surveying loaves of golden-brown bread. I see Papa in his library, staring thoughtfully into the fire. I look up into the black walnut tree that has grown so tall and broad in the years since we replanted. I have often leaned against it in the afternoons, sketching in its cool shade. Our animals are all gone now except for Obsidian, our proud black stallion that is harnessed to the cart, and he will need to be sold in Independence when we buy oxen to pull the loaded wagon on our journey next spring. But it is neither Obsidian nor Bertie and her calves that I fix in my memory now to take with me. It is Mattie, gone these five years, with her spritely, funny turn of head, still looking up at me in memory, ready for mischief.

*****

February 1, 1870 (A little more than four months later)

Alcove Spring, Kansas

We are completing the first day of our long journey to California. This morning at dawn, we left Independence, Missouri, the "jumping off point," as everyone in the wagon train strangely calls it, as if we were jumping off a riverbank into the water instead of plodding down a dirt trail. In Independence, we sold Obsidian to buy two sturdy oxen and provisions. We watched a while for the weather to warm a bit, which it did this week—right on cue by God's mercy, Papa says. I do not understand what God's mercy has to do with those clan bullies making us leave our home.

It is odd that we are already in another state now, but last night Paul showed me in his book of maps how Independence is right near the state border, so we woke up today in Missouri and will go to sleep in Kansas. Paul is having a high time mapping out our route.

It did not take long to leave the farms on the outskirts of Independence and to enter the wilderness. It is a little frightening, but mostly exciting. Papa, Mama, Paul, Amelia, Gus, and I are together, and I will not be afraid.

This evening, we have left the trail and gone about a mile to a campsite at Alcove Spring, where the spring becomes a beautiful waterfall that runs from rocks above into a pool below. Mama lets Paul strip off his dusty clothes and join the other boys in plunging into the icy pool. I can hear them splashing and laughing as I help Mama prepare supper. I wish I could join them, but since I am a girl I must be content with going later with the women to wash our hands, faces, and feet. The water is so cold that my skin tingles, but it is worth it to get the dust off my skin.

Our supper is simple—beans cooked with bacon and a few pieces of lettuce. Amelia says we should be grateful for the fresh vegetables we have brought from Independence, because it could be a long while before we taste the likes of them again.

It is an adventure to sleep outside on the ground. Papa and Paul put down tarps and cover them with the few blankets we have been able to carry with us in the scarce space available. This forms only a thin layer between my bones and the stony ground. As I lie first on my back, then on my side, trying to go to sleep, I am startled by barking in the hills beyond.

"How can there be dogs way out here?" I sit up to ask Paul, who is wrapped in a blanket nearby.

"They're not dogs, Tillie. They're coyotes. They look kind of like small, skinny, furry dogs. They run together in packs, and we're going to be able to sketch some, maybe even tomorrow."

"Do they eat people?"

Paul laughs. "Oh, all the time. Especially eleven-year-old girls who are trying to draw them."

I pummel his arm, which makes him laugh harder until I start laughing, too. When we get quiet again, we lie on our backs for a long time, looking at the stars sparkling in the black velvet sky where no town lights dim them. At last, I fall asleep thinking of Paul's book of strange western animals, and I dream of furry creatures like small, skinny dogs, romping together across the prairie like Paul and I are.

*****

February 1870 (Later that same month)

Somewhere in the middle of Kansas

Most people on the wagon train who can walk do, to stretch their legs and to make contact with the ground, they say, and that's fine for Paul and me sometimes. The seats next to the driver also have their own merits, since it is possible to look ahead from a height to discover the new terrain, and to be reassured that we are in the company of many wagons like ours, snaking their long line into the wilderness. But our favorite spot is the back opening of our wagon, where Papa has set up his wonderful carved table, the only piece of fine furniture we have brought with us as a sample of his work. It is the perfect size, small but with enough of a surface to spread out papers, and Papa has covered it with canvas and set it in front of two water barrels, so Paul and I can perch on the barrels and draw what we see. Papa even got brown paper from the butcher in Germantown before we left, so that we can make rough sketches and save our fine paper for finished work.

Riding in the back of our covered wagon, we are the masters of all we see. No one else we've talked with wants to ride inside a wagon, where every step of the oxen and every jolt of the wheels jostles a body with the roughness of this journey without roads. Paul and I do, though, because we know what can be seen from the back of a wagon.

We met the first new, wonderful creature only hours after we left Independence, Missouri. There are few benefits to rising before five in the morning, but one of them is that we can sometimes encounter animals that would be hiding in the light of day. That morning it was quite early, perhaps seven; the sun had just risen and frost was still on the ground. We passed the outskirts of town where there were farms with open, empty fields waiting for spring planting, and grazing cows and sheep. Then we came quite suddenly into open prairie. Paul is teaching me with his picture book about the dry prairie of flat grasslands reaching across Kansas and Nebraska. Many of the animals hide in the tall grasses, but we are lucky that all the wagons passing over this trail have flattened the grasses in a wide swathe, so that some adventurous creatures are revealed.

This first was a small creature, peeking out of a hole to the left as our wagon passed. He had a sleek head like a squirrel, but as he emerged from the hole, he revealed a body bigger than most squirrels—plump, and maybe two feet long, with light-brown fur fluffier than a squirrel's, and bright black eyes watching us with such curiosity that he scrambled up out of his hole and stood on two feet, like a little man. Then he held up his front paws to his chest like a pet dog begging for a treat. His tail was long and nearly as furry as a fox's, and tipped in black as a fox's is. We sketched him as fast as we could while the wagon jolted ahead slowly. The picture book told us that he is a prairie dog, and we have seen many like him this past week. Paul and I are glad for these creatures' fearlessness that brings them so close to our wagon. We have enough good sketches that we will surely be able to do some finished drawings later.

Though life on the trail has its discomforts, it also offers sweet freedom. As long as we do our chores, obey the rules, and keep moving with the wagons, our days and several hours of our nights are at our own command, and we have the chance to draw for long stretches without the interruptions of school or home projects. It was not so for those long months in Germantown near Memphis, while we waited for winter to come and go. There, our uncle was a dictator and we were all under his heavy shadow.

*****

October 1869

(About four months earlier)

Germantown near Memphis, Tennessee

"*Kinder, seid stille!*" Herr Schotter bellows, commanding us children to be still, which to him means absolutely still.

Paul and I have made the evidently horrible mistake of whispering to each other about the beautiful carpet, lamps, and paintings surrounding us. Papa flinches at our host's outburst, but then simply looks at us mildly and says nothing. We have visited the homes of neighbors often enough to know that Papa will not soon contradict the way a man manages his own home.

We are standing in the foyer of Mama's cousin, Tante Hilda, and Tante Hilda's husband, whom we have been strongly cautioned to address only as Herr Schotter. We have just arrived in Germantown to stay in safety from the clan bullies until we are able to leave for California in the spring. Mama and Amelia are hugging Tante Hilda, while Papa and Herr Schotter are shaking hands. Herr Schotter glares at Paul and me, perhaps waiting for us to tremble and cower as we will learn he has taught his own children to do. But Paul and I have not been taught to tremble or cower, and when we do not do so, it is clear that he does not approve. It seems to me that Herr Schotter would like for us children not only to be still, but to disappear into the air for good, and he is angry that we do not. "*Kinder auf irhe Zimmern!*" he calls to the servant, who bows and obediently begins to lead all the children off to our rooms as if leading animals to their pens so that the people—the adults—can carry on their business. Gus has been clasping my hand fearfully, and now he runs to Mama, who circles him with her arm.

Mama, never at a loss, chooses this moment not to argue, but to present each one of us to our relatives with exquisite politeness, and of course, in German. "*Moment mal, Anna. Herr Schotter, darf Ich vorstellen: unsere Tochter, Amelia; unser Sohn, Paul; unsere Tochter, Matilda; und unser jungsten Sohn, Augustus.*"

Paul bows slightly. I try to curtsey as gracefully as Amelia does, but I have neither her practice nor her natural grace, and I stumble a little. Gus hides his face in Mama's skirt.

Herr Schotter glares at me again, and then at Gus, but does not address us. "*Also, Sie haben viele Kinder,*" he says to Mama and Papa. "*Wir machen das Beste aus dieser Situation.*"

Now it is Papa who speaks, and in English this time, so even Gus understands. "Herr Schotter, we have always considered that to have these many children is the very best of situations." He looks from one to the other of us, delivering his love and protection. "I am sorry that you will not meet our eldest son Joseph, who is staying in Nashville for the time being."

Herr Schotter answers only, "Humph," and straightens himself, as Tante Hilda leads us, all of us, into the dining room for refreshments. Evidently, now that we have been presented formally, it is expected that we also should be entertained. My clever mama and my gentle papa have won a battle for us, but the struggle with the tyrannical husband of our aunt continues for four more months until we depart.

We live from day to day with Herr Schotter's vehement disapproval, and the house, when he is present, feels the way a prison must feel. We are compelled to be here, but we are neither wanted nor comforted by the one in authority. Anything we do—walking into the wrong room at the wrong time, being late to supper or being early to supper, taking a second helping of potatoes or not finishing our soup, smiling (which he interprets as insolence), or not smiling (which he calls sullenness)—anything can anger him and start his terrible shouting in German. At home, I loved the rich, strong sounds of the German language, but now I flinch at its harshness.

Herr Schotter does not hate children, Mama says, and he does not hate us. She and Tante Hilda are from Bavaria, a small and gentle part of Germany with much song and dance and *gemutlichkeit*, which is coziness. But Herr Schotter is Prussian. He is a strict and proud man, and we should respect him for his high principles. He was once in the Prussian army, and ever since then he has been concerned with military and political issues. Now he is a strong supporter of Kaiser Wilhelm I, and though he lives in America, his heart is still with the German Empire. So Mama says.

Herr Schotter is mean. I am not sure that he has a heart, and I wish he were still across the sea with the German Empire. So I say.

When Papa told us we would travel across the country to California, it was a shocking and fearful prospect, but still an exciting one, promising new adventures. Paul and I did not imagine these long months in a strange and unexciting place, though Papa did try to prepare us. As we drove from Nashville to Germantown, he explained again that the timing of our escape from the clan bullies was bad, that we could not leave for California in the fall because the journey would last for at least four months, and would take us into mountains that would be dangerous or even fatal to cross in winter. We would need to prevail upon the kindness of Tante Hilda and her family, and wait until at least February to join a wagon train in Independence, Missouri.

Although Tante Hilda is really Mama's cousin, we call her our auntie because she is like Mama's sister. Herr Schotter must never be called uncle, but only Herr Schotter, except by his wife, who calls him Rudi, and his children who, unbelievably, call him Herr Papa. Tante Hilda is strong like Mama, but she is harder. Mama is strong like the earth; she can be hard or giving depending on the circumstances. But Tante Hilda is hard like mountain rock. She addresses us politely, and makes sure we have food at the table and enough warm blankets for our beds, but she stays busy most of the time and rarely speaks with us children. I admire her because she seems to want to do what is right, but I would not want to have to disagree with her. Paul says that the difference in the two cousins is that Mama is Mama plus Papa, whereas Tante Hilda is someone like Mama, but added to Herr Schotter.

Their children, our second cousins, are Franz and Sissi. Paul had looked forward to knowing Franz, who is sixteen and almost a man, and they are becoming friends, but not of the adventure-seeking, wrestling, mock-fighting type that Paul had imagined. Franz is a different kind of boy.

When we can escape his parents, Franz takes his sister Sissi, Paul, and me on long walks along Cherokee Trace, which winds between the Wolf River and Noncannah Creek. We hike through dense woods of birch and hickory trees while the sun shines down through their leaves to create lacey shadows. When we reach the river, we inhale its rich, muddy scent and walk alongside the strong current fed by autumn rains. It is delicious to move our legs and arms, to talk and laugh freely, perhaps even more so because of the usually oppressive atmosphere of Herr Schotter's house .

We must walk slowly and take many rests, though, because Franz is sickly. When he was younger, the yellow fever came to Germantown. His little brother Karl died then, and his family feared that Franz would die, too. But Franz says he knew somehow that he had to stay alive, that he had something good to do with his life, and so he fought to live with all his will. As he recovered, he began to take short walks through the countryside and to write stories and poems set in the woods and by the river. He carries these poems on our walks and reads them to us as we perch on fallen logs and rocks to rest. Franz's words blend naturally with rustling leaves and flowing water and birdsong. Franz says that almost dying taught him to love life with a piercing love, and that is what a person must have to write well.

While Franz is gentle and entertaining, Sissi is like a princess in a fairy tale. When I tell her so, she laughs and says that she is named after a Bavarian princess who became an empress, and her name must have some magic that makes people think she is a princess, too. Sissi is fine and humble the way that a real princess is supposed to be. She seems always to think of what she can do for someone else. She is thirteen, and so pleasing to look at, with her golden hair, green eyes, and gentle round face, that I sketch her again and again in hopes that I can take the memory of her with me when we leave.

The first time we are alone together, the day after my family arrives, Sissi brings me to her room, takes from her wardrobe the loveliest blue muslin dress, and holds it out to me.

"Cousin Matilda, you have not been able to bring many dresses with you, I think. You must wear this to dinner." Her smile dimples her plump cheeks.

The dress is the blue of the sky at twilight on a late summer evening. It is like the blue dress I wore when I was little, when our lives were easier and Tod Carter would spin me in a circle and the skirt would bell out around me. I have not had a new dress since I can remember, but only Amelia's dresses made over to my size, and she prefers dark and stern clothing.

"What a beautiful color," I finally answer.

"Try it on. You are taller than I am but I am plumper than you are, so it should fit you," she says with a laugh.

It fits well. I accept the loan of the dress and take great care of it, but later she will not hear of my returning it. This is only the first of her thoughtful offerings, of her belongings and her gentle words, and especially of her company, which carries me through the long days when we are trapped inside the house and must watch our every word and act. How has it not crushed her to live all her life in the coldness and gloom of her father's house?

But Sissi is like the pansies that Mama used to plant in our garden, the ones that look delicate but bloom into early winter in spite of chilling blasts and little sunlight. She is strong enough that I can tell her some of what has been happening to my family and me in the past few years without frightening her or making her sad. She listens calmly and attentively and, when my words are spent, smiles and gives me tea and toast.

I wonder now what I gave Sissi in that exchange of our young hearts—hopefully something of value, perhaps a glimpse of a greater world beyond her castle walls. In any case, Sissi was my first close friend, and though we never saw one another again after this visit, I will never forget her.

After Sissi, I will have two lifelong friends, Rosa Bonheur, the great painter and advocate for women, and Count Ferenc Blaskovits, who will become my husband.

*****

September 1894
(Twenty-five years later)
Tata Castle, Hungary

I am strolling through the palace gardens bordering the lake, reveling in the cool breezes after almost unbearably hot summer months spent painting in Tangier. What a gracious host Earl Miklós Esterházy has been since my arrival here several days ago. We met in Tangier, and speaking English with him was so comfortable after the rigor of speaking French almost exclusively in recent years. The earl liked my paintings and invited me here to paint his dogs, but he has done much more, introducing me to many possible clients whose homes are in England and Austria-Hungary. He is a passionate admirer of dogs and horses, and is in agreement with me that they should be portrayed realistically, unsentimentally, in their natural dignity.

I will begin to sketch his dogs soon, but Earl Esterházy has insisted that I take a few more days to rest from the journey and the change in weather. As eager as I am to begin work, I can see that this is a wise suggestion. The doctors say that my lungs are weak, and this is why I so often suffer from colds and coughs. I have become so accustomed to the demands of work and travel, though, that today I must work at resting.

As I turn a corner of the garden path, a man approaches me, apparently with some purpose. He is of moderate height, trim, and dressed nicely, although not as formally as some of the palace guests. As he nears me, he sweeps off his hat to reveal dark hair streaked with silver, worn long to his chin. His warm brown eyes meet mine a brief moment before he bows from the waist.

"À votre service, Mademoiselle Bonheur," he greets me in French. "*Je m'apelle* Ferenc Blaskovits."

So this is Ferenc Blaskovits, the realist landscape painter. I have heard of him even in Paris and know that he is of the Hungarian nobility, but since I am unsure of his title, I consider it wise simply to curtsey slightly.

"*Monsieur*." I smile and extend my gloved hand, which he raises by the slightest touch of the fingertips and which he does not kiss, but over which he bows. Whether or not he is a member of the royal house, his manners are exquisite.

"Would you be comfortable speaking English, Monsieur?"

"But, yes, Mademoiselle. I do speak the English if you will like to be amused." His accent is as charming as his humor.

"You are a painter, Monsieur—and a realist painter, I believe?"

"And you are the American painter of true animals, as I know, Mademoiselle."

I am taken aback that he knows of my work, and no doubt I have shown that I am, since he gives a little laugh and bows again.

"Forgive me, Mademoiselle. We have just met, but I have wished to know you long times. Will you be kind to walk with me?"

I incline my head in agreement. His warmth has silenced me momentarily.

We stroll through the formal gardens past roses of every hue and perfume, still blooming vigorously in the mild autumn weather. I ask him about life in Hungary, and he describes the complex empire of many countries that is Austria-Hungary. He explains that when a very young man, he chose to avoid the demands of politics and to concentrate on making art. He speaks of his painting and of what he knows of mine, and we find that we share a commitment to realism founded in respect for the subjects of our work. I tell him about my papa, his courage and kindness, the beauty of his workmanship, about my brother Paul who was my first teacher, and about how inspired I am by Rosa Bonheur. As we meander back toward the palace, Ferenc stops beside a small tree of yellow roses, breaks one, and extends it to me with a bow.

"At this moment, Mademoiselle Lotz, I dare only to offer you the yellow rose of friendship, but this is not your true rose, not your true color. This I hope to learn in time."

So it begins—the walking and the talking that we will renew each time we meet, at first year to year, then day to day, and at last moment to moment, as our friendship takes root, branches out, and blossoms.

*****

October 1913
(Nineteen years later)

9 Rue de Campagne Premier, Paris

"This is a linden tree, Tillie," Ferenc explains as he digs a hole in our small garden in spite of my objections. "It is a symbol of peace and beauty."

"But, Ferenc, we are only renting here." I am shivering in the cold, wet wind that blows back my husband's hair from his leathery face. His hands and forearms are covered in wet soil as he continues to widen and deepen the hole. "We may not be able to stay. We may choose not to stay. As you have said so cleverly, we have learned to write with pencil in our date books."

"Yes, Tillie, this is true. But your brother Paul, he is a part of you, no?"

"He is, one of the best parts of me."

"Certainly, and though now he has gone, you still say of him, 'He *is*,' not 'He *was*.' This is also true, no?"

"It is true." The tears come again without warning, as they have for the past week. Ferenc says it is good that I am finally weeping now as I could not last month when I first heard that Paul was gone from this world, that I have passed from cold, dark grief into a warmer sorrow. It was so unexpected—Paul was only fifty-eight years old. His heart simply stopped—dear heart. I will not be there to bury his ashes next to Mama and Papa, so Ferenc is holding another kind of ceremony.

"He is one of the best parts of me," I say again, "and I will carry him with me."

"Good." Ferenc tenderly lifts the small sapling and kneels in the damp grass to ease it into its new home. "Then we plant the tree. And whether we stay or whether we go, the tree will stay, and it will live. Will you make steady the trunk while I finish preparing its new home?"

The trunk of the sapling is smooth, damp, cool. Ferenc spreads the roots over a mound of soil and fills the hole. Together we pat the earth firm with our palms. The wet, sharply sweet scent fills my nose.

"Now," Ferenc says, taking my muddied hand in his, "we pray. Our Father, we put this tree into the ground and you give it new life. Our brother Paul will be put into the ground. Give him new life."

"Amen," I answer, and for a moment I can see Paul's face as if he stood before me.

*****

March 1870 (Forty-three years earlier)

Just past Fort Hall, Idaho

Paul puts a reassuring hand on my shoulder. "Only a few more weeks," he mumbles sleepily. We are rising before dawn on yet another morning, cold and stiff from sleeping on the ground with nothing but a tarp and a few blankets. We have been on the trail for three months; the novelty and excitement have long since worn off, and the past several weeks have seemed eternity. We stumble to the water bucket, splash our faces, and join Mama, Papa, and Amelia at the fire.

"This, too, shall pass," Mama says, smoothing back my hair and handing me a cup of steaming coffee and a johnnycake dipped in molasses. The sweet cornmeal and strong, deliciously bitter coffee lift my spirits

"Indeed," Papa says. "We are making progress. Today all our California-bound wagons will head south as well as west, along the Raft River on our way to Nevada."

Paul pulls the treasured, dog-eared map from his pocket and he and Papa bend their heads over it until Paul is again inspired. We have been following "the mighty Snake River," as Paul calls it, for drinking water and fishing. Papa and Paul have become quite the fishermen, and take me along sometimes when Mama can spare me. Last week I hooked a trout more than a foot long and Paul slowly, patiently pulled back on the line to help me bring it in. That night at supper, my fish—with its crispy skin and mild, flaky meat—was more delicious than any I have tasted before or since.

Soon the Snake River will widen even more to meet the Raft River that flows south toward Utah and Nevada. This place is called "the Parting of the Ways," where the families heading for Oregon will follow the trail north and west, but we who are heading for California will go south and west through Idaho for a week or so, then cut across the very northwest tip of Utah to go southwest across Nevada. In Nevada we will need to cross a desert for forty miles, so we will take a few days of rest for ourselves and our animals, and fill every available vessel with water. Thankfully we will cross the desert in spring and not in summer, when we might not make it—Papa says that many have died trying. Paul has shown me a hundred times the route we are planning, detailing its adventure and its dangers. Today will be the day the wagon train splits in two.

Last night we had a sort of farewell party for the Parting of the Ways. We ate more delicious fresh fish, and used the last of the dried fruit to sweeten our johnnycakes. Some of the men drank a toast together, and the ones going to the California gold fields got very excited, telling everyone about all the gold they are going to discover and how rich they are going to be.

Gus, who is already eight but still a bit of a baby, asked Papa, "Are we going to California to get gold and live in a big house and have servants and ride in a fine carriage?"

"No, Gus, we don't need riches. We are going to California to be free to live our lives in peace, and that is worth more than any gold we could find."

Now, as we break camp and resume the trail, Paul tries to infect me with his enthusiasm, but it is a difficult enterprise. That is, until we spot the elk—the enormous, magnificent bull elk, eating grass at the edge of a woods in a valley below the trail. When he raises his head to chew, he appears bigger than two huge stallions—frighteningly big even at a distance. Judging from his relation to the trees behind him, he is probably about ten feet tall, with antlers spreading as wide as my height of four and a half feet. He does not seem disturbed by our wagons, and so far none of the men or boys has tried to shoot at him. Paul and I grab pencil and paper, sketching as swiftly as ever we can.

I have learned that with a large animal it is important to sketch first all of the muscles and underlying bone structure. The elk's powerful muscles run in great ropes within his flanks and thighs. Once I have a suggestion of these, I can look at his coat of short fur, like a deer's, which is russet brown, with patches of lighter fur on his back and around his brown eyes.

"His mate is probably in the woods," Paul says, "either pregnant or with her young, while the bull is bold enough to come out for food and to look out for danger."

"Could our wagon train be a danger that would make them run away?" I ask, still looking intently from elk to paper to elk.

"Of course, but we are too high above for him to smell or hear us. It's the perfect vantage point to draw from."

"I wish we could draw the female and the young, a whole family."

"Let's be happy with what we have, eh? If we hadn't been forced to leave home, we wouldn't have dust in our noses and throats, and we wouldn't be so tired from the early mornings and long days, and we wouldn't be weary to death of jostling along in this wagon and looking at what often seems desolation, right?"

I nod in commiseration.

"But we also would never have seen or drawn such a creature as this elk."

I take my eyes from my drawing for an instant to look, really look, at Paul, the strong bones of his face so like Papa's, his forthright blue eyes, and his joy, which he somehow finds in himself more than in his experiences. This face I do not need to draw. It is imprinted on my heart.

*****

AUGUST 14, 1880

(TEN YEARS LATER)

San Jose, California

Tomorrow, very early, I will leave our home to study at *L'Académie de Peinture de Paris.* It is impossible to explain the strong emotions competing in me, but they create a force of energy pushing me into my new life.

The distance is great, and the journey will be long. I will take the Transcontinental Express Train from San Francisco to New York City. This is advertised as taking eighty-three hours, or a little less than four days and three nights. I will have a sleeping compartment on the train and take my meals in the dining car. How different this will be from my last journey across the country in our covered wagon only ten years ago.

In New York, I will stay with a friend of Mrs. Phoebe Hearst, wife of William Randolph Hearst. I am so grateful for everything she has done for me—the paintings she has commissioned, the patrons she has introduced, and most of all the way she has believed in my talent and my ability to use it. I recall her advice when we last met.

"Matilda, you have said that you want to paint, and you have established that you can. Do not be content to become what they call 'an accomplished woman.' This is the stereotype of the charming dilettante who holds court in her parlor. Rather, marshal your will and all your talent to become a painter, a good painter. Being a woman or a man has little to do with it."

This is my commission.

Two days after I arrive in New York, I will embark on an ocean voyage that could take eight days or more depending on the weather. This will be an unprecedented adventure, dangerous in a way different from crossing the country in a covered wagon—not too little water but so very much water that the ship labors to navigate. Still, when I was out on the Monterey Bay on a small ship I enjoyed it very much; the captain said I got my "sea legs" quickly.

When we reach Paris, I will be met by another friend of Mrs. Hearst's who will help me to get settled in a room near *L'Académie*. My classes will begin about two weeks after that, in mid-September, so I will have the delicious opportunity to become acquainted with Paris.

It will be very hard to say good-bye to Mama and Papa, especially because I do not know when I will see them again, but I have expected this since I am a woman now and must make my own life. But Paul—I cannot yet imagine life apart from the brother who has shared everything with me these many years. I try to tell him this after supper as we sit in the backyard, looking at the stars together one last time.

"Now, don't go getting sentimental, Tillie. You are about to have the time of your life. This is what you have always wanted and always prepared for. You are going to be an artist."

"Will you come to visit me in Paris?"

"You'll just have to get really successful and rich and send me the money for the trip."

"What about you, Paul? Are you going to get successful and rich?"

"Sure, Tillie. I'm doing just fine at the photography studio. I will be able to make a good living at it. What I've never told you before, though, and what I've known almost all along is that you are in a different league than I am. No, don't argue. It's a fact. I don't mind it at all. You can be a great painter, Tillie, so go be great. Work hard, be brave, and don't let anything stop you. And one more thing, Tillie. Try to find peace. It's hard for people with great talent to find peace. It's hard for you."

At this moment, I am not really listening to what he is saying. I am looking at his wonderful face and thinking of who he is to me. "You have taught me so much, Paul. You have helped me learn to see. I would not be going to Paris if not for you."

Paul puts his arm around my shoulder and we sit in silence for a while, looking up into a sparkling sky. "Go to bed now, Tillie," he says at last. "Morning will be here soon and you have a life ahead of you."

*****

October 1883
(Three years later)
Paris

It is raining, of course—it is nearly always raining—but I must drive into the country regardless. I paint animals, I tell myself, and the animals I am currently sketching are to be found only in the country—a small flock of sheep in a meadow. But both my mind and my body resist working in the rain. I know that the moment my driver helps me from the carriage my boots and skirts will be soaked by the watery mud of the road. As uncomfortable as it will be to sketch all day in wet boots, I can accept this, perhaps because it is unavoidable. What is worse, what annoys me to no end, is being weighed down and chilled by layers of skirts that become yet more sodden as I traipse across the meadows.

For whom must I so attire myself? My humble, kind driver, a farmer whose wife no doubt pins up her skirts to accomplish her own work in the wet fields?

And I wonder, if Rosa Bonheur were here beside me right now, would she laugh and chide me for my slavery to convention? She would. *She* would do what best serves her work, and always has done. Her famous practices of wearing men's clothing and cutting her hair short were born of simple need: no woman was allowed to enter the slaughterhouses, so she masqueraded as a man in order to study the animals' anatomy.

I can hear her deep, authoritative voice as if she were standing beside me: "*Ma chère fille*, think first what is good for the work. This is the norm for your every choice."

Suddenly I know exactly what to do. I have no men's trousers, and truth be told I would not dare to don them if I had, but from the box on my dressing table, I take a handful of pins and begin hitching up my skirts as boldly as any good French farm wife. Today, I tell myself, this lady's skirts will stay dry and her damp stockings will soon dry in the breeze as she draws.

Indeed, they do.

*****

April 1889
(Six years later)
Ecouen, France

I am writing a letter:

Dear Paul,

I can hardly wait until you arrive in July, and I spend all my spare time preparing for your visit. We will have Bastille Day on the fourteenth, and Paris will be most exciting for you.

I have now taken a studio and rooms at Ecouen, a little village near Paris. The country round about is pretty for backgrounds, and as the village is built on a hill the views are very fine. Nearby is a handsome castle. I am sorry to say I could not finish my picture for the year's Salon. I started a canvas of four oxen and spent considerable time upon it, but unfortunately for me, the farmer could not spare his oxen any longer, just at the time when I most needed them to finish my picture. It is too late to start another. I feel bad, for my friends will expect to see some of my works at the exposition. It is difficult to paint animals that farmers use for their work. One loses so much time with them, and ought to own the animals to be able to study them well.

I have been making studies of plowed ground for my picture. There is nothing more difficult to paint, as the light and even color changes every few minutes. The sky effects here are beautiful, and at this season dark stormy clouds fill the sky. Sometimes I get the benefit of them and come home like a drowned rat; in fact, I have to work in the rain half the time.

Yes, I still complain a great deal, but as you remind me always, I am doing exactly what I choose.

Come soon.

Yours,
Tillie

*****

DECEMBER 1894
(FIVE YEARS LATER)

Paris

Rosa Bonheur and I are taking tea in my Paris rooms, and I am sharing with her a newspaper article praising my painting, *A Street in Cairo*, being shown in the San Francisco Ladies' Art Exhibition. But it is not my painting that concerns Rosa.

"This exhibition is good, I think," Rosa says. "In San Francisco, many women are *sérieuses* about their art, and critics now recognize them. It is good for women in Europe, too, and everywhere. Does this paper talk of the statue of Queen Isabella by Harriet Hosmer?"

"Oh, yes," I answer, scanning the article. "Yes, here it is. The statue was commissioned by the Isabellas in Chicago last year, to give the Queen equal credit with Columbus for discovering America. It is being displayed before the twenty-three-foot Pampas Palace. Well, critics and public alike praise the statue, but the Isabellas women's group is suffering quite a bit of resistance toward their message. It seems that it took weeks of negotiation to find a good place for the statue at the exhibition."

"*Domage.* A shame. But of course there is *la résistance.* Isabella is the symbol of the woman who has power and influence. Very frightening for the little people. This is *difficile* for Harriet Hosmer, to mix art with politics. She must be *sérieuse*, but at the same time she must laugh at *la résistance*, as I do. If she does not, she loses her heart and cannot work."

"But, Rosa, I never mix art with politics. I have no desire to do anything but paint. Sometimes I wonder whether that is selfish."

"*Non! C'est bon, ma chère.* This is good. This is your *personnage.* You are a private person. But if you are true to yourself, you help our cause."

Rosa is different from me in so many ways. Her presence is large and often fierce. She challenges people to open their minds. Though painting is her first commitment, as it is for me, she has others that she is almost as passionate about. Yet she has never even suggested that I should try to imitate her, but has always paid attention to supporting my own strengths. In these years of separation from my mama in California, Rosa has been like a mother to me, sharing her greater life experience, teaching me to focus on what is essential.

*****

September 1890 (Four years earlier)

Rosa Bonheur's Chateau at By

The air is cool and crisp, beginning to tinge the oak leaves with red, gold, and orange even as the sun warms our faces. We are strolling through Rosa's private zoological gardens where we can see to either side of a tree-lined path not only deer, gazelles, and shaggy ponies from Iceland, but wild boar, and even a lion who is so well fed he simply regards us mildly from a distance. It is a marvel to be here, a marvel to paint here in the company of so great a painter. But at this moment, we are resting from our work and Rosa is regaling me with her stories.

"All of Paris was talking of me behind their hands, behind their fans…"

"Behind your back, we say in English."

"*Oui*, this, too. And the *notoriété* was worth the *problèmes*. I was selling many paintings. *The Horse Fair* became *famouse*, and the English Queen Victoria invited me to London."

"Did you wear men's clothing to meet the Queen?"

She ignores my teasing tone, stops in her tracks, and faces me gravely. "There was no need to wear the men's clothing for Queen

Victoria. She is a woman, and a queen. She understands what I do. *Ma chère*, I am the living art. My short hair, my trousers, my cigar, these say to the world: 'If I must behave as a man to be treated as his equal, then so I shall.' Why say this to a woman who knows that she can rule an empire, and does?"

"I see...but I am not great as Queen Victoria is, or as you are, and I shall never be so. My paintings might become great; they are very well received. But I myself do little but paint, and that does not make me interesting. Am I fulfilling my potential, Rosa?"

She grasps me by both arms and speaks into my eyes. "Ah, *ma chère*, to be great, as you say, this is not *l'idée importante. Non. Avoir le courage de vos convictions!* Have the courage of your beliefs, Tillie! Live them. This is *l'idée importante.* Make true art. If this makes you *famouse—bien—*this is good. If not, this is also good. To be great is no *objectif.* It is only a result."

I nod, beginning to understand. "My papa had the courage of his convictions when he would not take sides in the war, even though it was dangerous, and when he refused to give in to the Ku Klux Klan. And when he started making beautiful furniture and instruments again and again no matter what happened to stop him."

"*Oui.* And as you do when you go where you need to go and paint what you see. You are *la fille* of your father."

"Yes, I am my father's daughter. It makes me happy to hear you say so."

"I know this is so. I am also my father's daughter. He taught me to make art and not to be afraid. This is what kept you at *l'Académie*, even when it was *très difficile, non*?"

We exchange a knowing look and laugh together like soldiers after a difficult battle won. A battle that was indeed during my first year at *L'Académie*, one in the midst of which I could not laugh.

*****

September 1880
(Ten years earlier)

L'Académie de Peinture de Paris

What am I doing here in this strange country with its strange language, here in this studio, in this sea of young men who are staring at me, not bothering to hide their curiosity and scorn? How am I to function here?

My teachers at the San Francisco School of Design have believed in me, believed I was ready to study in Paris. Kind Mr. Virgil Williams of the San Francisco Art Association has had the confidence to fund my tuition and expenses. But that was in America, a young country, a hopeful and possible country. This—this is Paris, for many centuries a city of great painters, and I am a twenty-one-year-old woman, apparently the only woman in my class.

Our professor enters and welcomes us to our course of study. He speaks briskly in French. Though I can understand only a little, I gather that we will not sketch today indoors, but tomorrow in the countryside. Today we have a visiting artist, one who is very successful in depicting the realistic nature scenes we will study, Monsieur

Emile Van Marcke. He enters, stately with full white beard, a broad forehead, and a tuft of white hair.

Monsieur Van Marcke advises us to work first with our eyes to see, and only then with our hands to portray. Of the paintings he shows us, both his own and others', I very much admire his *Cows in a Meadow*, the brindled cows and sweet white calf walking toward the viewer with such movement and life, a little black dog flanking them. Perhaps one day, if I work very hard, I shall be able to study with him privately, and to learn to show such movement in a painting.

As class closes and we file to the door, one young man breaks from the group of gawkers and approaches me. He is tall and dark in the French manner, with large brown eyes. He might be handsome if his face were not so marred by insolence and a mean spirit.

"*Mademoiselle, es-tu perdu?*" he addresses me insultingly in the familiar form, with a mocking bow. "*Puis-je t'aider?*" He is asking whether I am lost, and whether he may direct me. His friends snicker in their little clique.

My face becomes hot, my breathing quickens, and the old shaking feeling comes over me. I do not answer, not only because I do not yet trust my command of the language, or of my temper, but more so because he does not deserve a reply. I meet his stare and breeze past him through the door. Fuming with rage, I walk home so quickly I barely see my surroundings. When I arrive at my rooms the only possible recourse is to paint. I don my smock and begin to create a sky such as I remember from September mornings in Franklin. Under it I intend to place Bert who will walk toward the viewer in the lively manner of Emile Van Marcke's cows. As I lose myself in mixing Prussian blue with white until it is the perfect shade of clear morning light, it slowly occurs to me that the rudeness of those young men has in fact done me a service. It has posed an important question that I am gaining the clarity to answer. Am I lost? No, I most certainly am not. I am once again among hostile men, again challenged, but I am in Paris, a city of painters, and I am becoming a painter in spite of anything they can say or do.

*****

September 1874
(Six years earlier)
San Francisco

"No, sir, I am not in the wrong room," I answer Professor Virgil Williams, who is to be my new teacher at the California School of Design. "I am learning to paint. I am your new pupil, sir. Matilda Lotz."

Mr. Williams looks baffled, and the students, nearly all young men though all older than my fifteen years, whisper and laugh.

"Silence, pupils. Continue your sketches while I make some inquiries." He leaves the room, leaves me standing in front of these unwelcoming strangers. I glance around the studio and soon forget the other students when I notice the model, a woman seated on a raised platform at the center of the room. She is draped in a white, Grecian-style garment with her hair piled atop her head to expose bare white shoulders, arms, and throat. She points a graceful bare foot, and her ankle and part of her calf extend from her skirts. I have never before seen so much of another human body. It is exquisite, and I want to draw it.

A young woman also a few years older than I am rises and walks toward me. Her palms are dark and shiny with pencil rubbings. She is smiling politely, and her face looks intelligent and well-intentioned.

"I am Ella Hopps," she says, "but you may call me Nellie. Why don't you take a seat until Professor Williams returns?" She gives her head a toss. "Pay no attention to these unmannerly children," she continues at a volume meant for their ears. "They know so few ladies of any sort, and we ladies who draw confuse them."

I nod and smile my thanks, sitting toward the outside of the circle of students, who eventually lose interest in me and return to their work. Hoping that I will have some time to complete a sketch, I take my tablet and pencils from my satchel and begin to look carefully at the model's feet, making first a few tentative strokes, and then sketching in earnest.

I have no idea how long I have been working when Professor Williams returns and approaches me.

"Miss Lotz," he begins, "I must apologize. I was not apprised of your joining our class. I understand that Mrs. Hearst has sponsored you here."

A buzz of whispers rises from the students. Mr. and Mrs. Randolf Hearst are greatly respected in San Francisco society, and I am very grateful that they have taken an interest in my drawing. Evidently, their patronage may help me to get along in class, too.

"But I see you have already begun." He nods his approval of my initiative, takes the sketch from my hands, and studies it. "This is not bad, Miss Lotz. You have shown judgement in beginning with a small study of the feet, and for the most part your lines are accurate. Look here, the curve of the heel is so. Here the shading needs to be adjusted. And there." He guides my hand through the corrections. "Very well. Carry on."

Now the room is silent and all eyes are upon me again. I do not learn why until later, when Nellie Hopps explains that today is the first time this school year that Professor Williams has expressed even qualified approval of a student's sketch. I cannot wait to tell Paul.

*****

Late February 1870 (Four years earlier)

Five or so miles past New Fort Kearny on the Platte River, Nebraska

I grasp Paul's arm and whisper, "Look! To your left—is it a wolf?" Paul nods, and without taking our eyes from this long-awaited wonder we grab pencils and paper from their place at our feet in the back of the wagon. For several moments I study the wolf's lean, taught muscles, his sleek, silvery fur, his princely head that has never bowed to a master. His ears are laid back, listening to us as intently as we are watching him. Then tentatively, I sketch and look again, sketch and consider, compare my lines with the lines of that masterful body. But his form is only the beginning; his fur is not really silver as it first appears, but as if two coats, an undercoat of white with an overcoat of gray and black that is luminous in the waxing morning light. And his eyes! Even from our distance they appear golden, and he does not take them from us. He neither approaches nor retreats, but simply observes our many lumbering wagons. I am thankful that we are on the outer rim of the wagons, thankful that our family's is at the end so that we can continue to behold him while we drive away. As his figure grows smaller and smaller and Paul and I sketch from his image burned on our memories, I think there is no better place to draw than our perch at the back of the wagon.

We have just some hours ago left New Fort Kearny, where we all have rested in the shelter of the fort and feasted on eggs, milk, and fresh bread. Not only are Paul and I energized for a day of drawing this new wonder, but the rifle-bearing men and boys of the wagon train have been too full of food and too distracted by the other comforts of our rest stop to see the wolf first and to shoot him, as they have often shot coyotes and other smaller creatures.

By the end of the day, both Paul and I have completed a sketch to our liking, and have stashed it safely away to paint when we reach our new home.

*****

April 17, 1870
(Two months later)

San Jose, California

"Mama, look!" As our dusty, battered wagon slows in front of a tidy white house at 684 2nd Street in San Jose, I have spotted something that will please my travel-weary mama.

"It's a castle with a tower!" Gus says.

In fact, the house does have a sort of tower, but there is time enough to see the house. I jump from the wagon, take Mama's hand, and pull her after me to the side yard, to the roses—deep-red roses with large, full heads and a wonderful perfume.

"Oh, Tillie," Mama sighs, cupping one large bloom in her palm and bending to breathe the fragrance. "How perfect. These are a different variety from the red roses we had in Franklin, but just as lovely. So early in the year and they are already blooming—what a wonder is this California climate."

I hug Mama, glad that something of beauty can give her pleasure again, and we join Papa and the others to climb the front stairs and enter the house itself. The front room is spacious and clean, with light streaming through its windows. It is also quite small, though, and entirely empty.

"This is not the fine home I once built for you, Margaretha," Papa says quietly.

"But it is also not damaged by bullets and cannonballs, and you are not damaged by tar and feathers," Mama answers, taking his hand. "We will make it a good home."

Mama and Papa have bought this house with gold they exchanged for in Independence, Missouri, and that is why we can afford to buy property at all after the expenses of the journey. Gold is really valuable, and people like it better than regular money in these days after the Civil War. Now, as I have gathered from what I have overheard, we have almost no money left at all, and we must live very simply for a while until Papa builds his business again.

Still, to have arrived here is something to celebrate. We will stay in this new place, and not be on the trail anymore. After we made it across the Forty Mile Desert, the rest of the trip seemed easy, at least to Paul and me. When we had reached Carson City, Nevada, we were almost in California, and California would be home. Papa said it used to be difficult and dangerous to cross the Sierra Nevada Mountains, but now that there are good toll roads, the going is much easier. We travelled late enough in the spring that we didn't have to deal with snowstorms, though once as we descended a mountain into a wet valley, the rain came down in torrents with lightning and thunder—nearly as beautiful as it was frightening—and we stopped right there on the road to shelter in the wagon until it was over.

The farther south and west we journeyed, though, the warmer the spring days became. From Sacramento to San Jose, we passed through valleys of wildflowers I had never seen before. I especially liked the tall, brilliant blue and pink ones that look like bunches of grapes turned upside down—fields and fields of them just as we descended from the mountains. Paul and I saw, and of course drew, prong-horned antelope with their stark white and brown coats, black horns, and black face markings, as well as so many birds of prey—hawks, eagles, and owls. I think we will be busy for many months completing drawings of all these new creatures sketched along the trail, and to paint them all could keep us busy for years. But once we were in California the thrill of the journey had passed, and our thoughts turned toward the promise of a home.

Now our life in San Jose begins. The few belongings we unload from the wagon do little to fill the empty rooms, and we will be both sitting and sleeping on the floor for many weeks while Papa makes us some furniture. But Papa and Paul have caught a rabbit, and Mama and Amelia have built a fire in the kitchen to make a stew, while Gus chases a neighbor's cat and Paul and I gather some volunteer lettuce from the abandoned kitchen garden in the backyard.

Paul walks over to me and takes my hand. "Close your eyes and come with me," he says, leading me stumbling across the yard. "Keep them closed," he says, easing me down to a sitting position on the lawn. "Now, breathe."

My head fills with a pungent freshness, sharp and clean like pine needles, only subtler, with a trace of sweetness. "That's rosemary," he says. "It's for remembrance, remember?"

I remember reading *Hamlet* together under the oak tree in our Franklin home last summer, though it seems decades ago. I remember the rosemary bush we planted from a cutting that Mrs. Carter gave us, and how we would smell it and quote from the speech Ophelia gives about the herbs after her heart and mind have broken. Suddenly a familiar shaking comes over me, and a dark bitterness.

"I remember, Paul. I remember *Hamlet*, and then the clan bullies. And before that I remember the battle, and Mattie, and the little drummer boy and Tod Carter. It's all inside me, Paul, and it won't go away and it takes the place of being happy. I remember everything."

"Tillie, I thought you would like it—"

"I know you did, and I am sorry, Paul. I would like to think of just the good memories, but they are all mixed up with other ones that are like horrible weeds, choking them. I would like to be happy inside like you are, but I am not."

"You are never happy, Tillie?"

"Sometimes. Being with you and Papa and Mama. Drawing."

Paul puts his arm around my shoulder and I lean my head against his. We sit that way for a long while until Amelia calls us to help with dinner.

*****

August 1870 (Four months later)

San Jose, California

Paul has done odd jobs for neighbors this summer and earned enough money for some oils, which he insists are not his, but ours. Because our new house is small and we have not yet found a place inside where the smell of the oils will not bother our family, we paint outdoors for now.

The yard is small, too, with only two trees, a live oak that is shorter than the Tennessee oaks and a Japanese maple that is of a medium height. These two modest trees are very important to Paul and me, because we are able to paint in their shade.

Paul has been working on a painting of an eagle in flight, and today I am putting the finishing touches on *The Wolf*, which I think is the best sketch I captured on our journey across the country. I understand this creature. He is part of a pack and loyal to them, but in my painting he is also a lonely hunter who has to be very strong.

*****

November 1870 (Three months later)

San Jose, California

"Matilda Lotz," the teacher says, breaking my concentration. "What is the product of this problem?"

I study the problem on the board, trying to solve it as quickly as possible, but there is no time. I have no doubt the teacher has already worked the problem and given the answer.

"You are failing yet again to pay attention, Matilda. What is it that is distracting you this time?"

My heart races as she approaches my desk and takes in her hand the drawing I have been making of our beautiful new horse Rolf—in the margins of my arithmetic book. No doubt she will scold me, but at least I know that she will not take this drawing from me as she has when she has caught me sketching on loose paper. She will want me to keep the book.

"You have defaced your book, Matilda," she says, scowling.

"Yes, ma'am."

"Why would you do such a thing?"

I look up, wanting to tell her how Rolf, such a great luxury for us but one Papa needs to visit clients, has occupied my every thought since Papa brought him home last week. Wanting to explain how attending school and doing homework take up so much of my time that I scarcely find an opportunity to draw during the week. Wanting to say how boring this arithmetic is. But she will not understand, so I am silent.

"Matilda, I want an answer from you. Why have you drawn in your arithmetic book?"

"I am out of paper, ma'am."

"What? You are out—you should not be drawing during class!"

Again I am silent.

"I will have to take this matter to your parents."

"Yes, ma'am."

It does not worry me that she will speak with Papa and Mama, who already know that I draw whenever I possibly can—in class, during recess, for a few stolen moments on a sidewalk bench on the way to or from school. I draw animals, mainly—our pigs, our chickens, our cow, and the neighbors' dogs. I like to invent new animals, too—to picture a calf with wings that can rise up into the sky like an eagle, or a wolf so tiny that it can fit in the palm of my hand. This is all so much more interesting than multiplication.

I have been in school for more than two months now, and it is not really bad, except for all the time it steals from drawing. Some of the stories we read are wonderful, and we also study the history of the United States before the war hurt it so much. I have met some new friends, too. They like to see my drawings and come to visit our animals from time to time on the way home from school. Mama and Papa, especially Mama, insisted that I resume my long-interrupted studies, since I am not needed at home this fall so much as I was over the summer.

The summer was very busy with settling into our new home. Papa began almost at once with a business of making and tuning pianos, and he has earned money enough that we have begun to furnish our house. When not working for a client, Papa bought wood to make beds, chairs, and a table. Mama, Amelia, and I spent long hours sewing featherbeds, linens, and curtains, and when the tinker came through town, Mama bought a few more pots, pans, and kettles. In time, Papa will be able to make another piano for us, and Amelia can play and give lessons again. Dear Papa understands that we all must make our art.

I am counting on his understanding the next day when my teacher raps on the front door, and he, Mama, and she disappear behind the closed parlor door. Of course, in this small house, it is very easy to hear their conversation from my perch on the stairs, where Paul, as ever, comes to join me.

"This obsession with drawing is hurting Matilda's education," says Miss Simms. "Why, just yesterday I discovered her drawing a horse in the margin of her arithmetic book!"

A gentle laugh escapes Papa. "Was the drawing good?"

"Was…? Mr. Lotz, your daughter is not focusing on her arithmetic."

"Indeed. Forgive me, Miss Simms. Naturally that is your chief concern, and it is an important one. Matilda must read and write and do figures, without a doubt. But you see, Matilda has a gift for drawing, and to ask her not to draw is like asking a bird not to sing."

"But how do you expect me to enforce discipline in my classroom when she is not attending to the lesson?"

"Yes, you must keep order in your classroom. Is Matilda distracting the other students?"

"Well, not exactly…"

"What would happen if she were allowed to draw, on paper of course and not in her book, and to listen to the lesson at the same time? I believe she would be able to do this if you would allow it."

"But I have never heard of such a thing. It is so unruly."

"Perhaps. But if Matilda promises to listen to the lesson and to draw only in quiet moments, will you agree to it?"

Silence. I suppose that silence is better than an argument.

After what seems a long time, Miss Simms replies, "Very well. We will try this idea of yours. But if she is unable to answer questions as the other students do, it will have to stop."

The moment I hear the door close, I fly down the stairs to hug Papa.

"Thank you, dear Papa, thank you! I shall not be a school mistress or a secretary, Papa. I shall draw and paint always."

"If you are to be an artist, my Tillie, you must be an educated woman, as well, able to keep your accounts, able to read difficult documents and great literature, able to write clearly and express yourself strongly."

"Yes, Papa. I promise to listen to the lessons as I draw. I can do it." I hug him more tightly and he rests his dear head on top of mine.

*****

AUGUST 1872 (TWO YEARS LATER)

San Jose, California

I have entered my painting of Mattie in the Santa Clara County Fair, and it has won a blue ribbon. It is a very small painting, ten inches square, and I was only seven when I painted it, but I still think it is the best work I have done so far because of how I knew her, how I could see her. Technique is important, of course, and now that I am thirteen I see that this painting has a lot of flaws, but it also has a lot of truth, and that is more important. I missed Mattie so much then and I would bring her back in my imagination. I imagined that it was a summer morning and I had just rolled down the hill leading to her pasture to surprise her with a hug. She turns her pert head to look back at me the way she always did. If a calf could laugh, this look would be Mattie laughing.

*****

DECEMBER 28, 1877 (FIVE YEARS LATER)

San Francisco, California

The Art Association has awarded me first prize for my oil painting, *Coyotes on the Prairie*. This is because Mr. Virgil Williams has been a strict and good teacher. He does not give compliments, but always challenges me to do better. When I first arrived at the California School of Design three years ago, I was very possessive of my ideas and their expression. I wanted to learn, of course, but I did not want to change the work I was doing. Mr. Williams has taught me to hold onto my vision but be willing to revise the execution of it on the canvas, to make it better and better until it is the best I can achieve.

One day last year I was painting a pack of coyotes from a sketch I had made on our family's journey across the country. This sketch meant the world to me because I had done it out in the wild, in the wonder of discovering these new creatures, and with Paul at my side.

"Miss Lotz, you should not go any further with your painting until you correct your sketch."

"Correct it, sir?" I asked, stricken.

"Look carefully at the coyotes' proportions. Are they accurate?"

I was there on the prairie with them, I wanted to say. They were only twenty feet away from me. Have you ever even seen a pack of coyotes on the prairie? Thankfully, I restrained myself.

"I did the sketch on the prairie, sir."

"I see. And you were how old?"

"Twelve, sir," I answered, at once recognizing that I would need to improve on a sketch done by a twelve-year-old child on the back of a moving wagon.

When I narrated the story that night at home, Papa explained that Mr. Williams was using the Socratic Method. Instead of telling me, Mr. Williams asked me questions, and as I answered I discovered the answers.

"What do you suggest, sir?"

"I would go to the library and find photographs of coyotes on the prairie. Sketch them, keeping in mind what you saw on that occasion more than what you drew. Paint from that sketch."

The painting is good. Even more importantly, I have learned that the willingness to accept critique and to revise is one of the qualities that distinguishes a professional artist from an amateur.

*****

October 21, 1897
(Twenty years later)
Tata Castle, Hungary

It is pleasant to be here again, enjoying the kind hospitality of Earl Miklós Esterházy who has become my patron and who has made his castle a home to which I can continue to return to rest from my travels. Today he is escorting me to the edge of his gardens, where he says there is a surprise for me.

"You have been very good to paint as you do, Matilda, so Szent Miklós has brought you a present," he says playfully.

"St. Nicholas is early with his gift."

"Yes, he knows you will need it before Christmas. Here we are."

In the meadow stands a small house built to look like the castle, with yellow walls, a red tile roof, and many tall windows.

"It is lovely, but I do not understand."

"This is your studio, Matilda. Here you will paint animals so that all can see what fine creatures they are."

I am speechless for a moment. "I cannot express my thanks for such a gift, St. Nicholas."

Of course I want to begin working right away, now that I have a fine new studio in a clearing where morning light pours through the windows of the eastern wall and afternoon light through the windows of the western wall. Earl Miklos insists that I take another day or two to renew my strength, though, and he is right, I do need a rest.

It has taken courage to work in the dirty streets of Cairo in the glaring sun. Flies swarmed over the subjects until I hired a local man to beat them off so that I could get at least an occasional glimpse of the animals' natural lines. In spite of all obstacles, the year in Cairo was very productive. I painted for dear life, not knowing when I would be able to return, and I finished four paintings, two of which have already sold. I think I will keep *Woman Driving Her Sheep*. I was able to capture the stunning light for that one, not only the radiance infusing the blue of the sky, but the light as it is cast on the old stucco walls. It is the uniqueness of the light that keeps drawing me back to Egypt and Africa, and I want to be able to look at it often when I am elsewhere.

It seems that I am always on my way elsewhere, which is exhilarating, and exactly what I want, but at times exhausting. I had just returned here to rest after the year of vigorous work in Egypt when Earl Miklos introduced me to the duke and duchess of Portland. They admired my paintings of the earl's dogs, and commissioned me to paint their famous horses. They were eager to have me start, so within a short week, I was on my way to Welbeck Castle in Nottingham.

This was my first visit to England, and I found the architecture majestic, though the weather was quite cold and damp. I chose to sketch outside in the pasture so that the horses could have freedom of movement. I needed to see their muscles in motion, and observe the particular character of each animal, which would not be possible in the confines of a stable. The price of authenticity in this case was a head cold that kept me in bed for several days, but it was worth the discomfort. I did indeed capture the nature of each of the horses, St. Simon and Donovan, and spent the following winter months happily transferring my good sketches to the canvas in a snug drawing room where a fire was kept burning. I am pleased with both paintings.

Now, after a brief return to Egypt, I am commissioned to paint Earl Esterházy's horses, a prospect I am looking forward to. To paint such a noble beast as a horse, to concentrate on the intelligent face, to spend time getting to know him uplifts my spirits. Horses make good company. I am considering the fact that it is mid-autumn, though, and I will take care to wear warm clothing while I sketch.

Last evening, Count Ferenc Blaskovits came to dinner at the earl's palace, and we had much to discuss. He has been painting in Morocco, and his *Danza des Dervisci* has been very well reviewed. We talked about the quality of the African light as well as the plague of the flies. He was amused that I actually hired someone to drive them from my subjects, and we found many other common experiences to compare.

Since we last met two years ago, Count Blaskovits has become ever more committed to realism and he complimented me on my success in portraying truth in nature. He actually said "portraying absolute truth in nature," which I had to deny, since who could do that? For nearly forty years, I have been trying with all my capacity simply to see absolute truth. To portray it would have to be a divine act, not a human one. Count Blaskovits and I share a common aesthetic, but I see that he is much more idealistic than I am, speaking and painting more expansively, more sweepingly.

Count Blaskovits has invited the earl and his entire party to his family's Budapest home next weekend. He will escort us to the opera to see Puccini's *La Boheme.* I have accepted with pleasure, but I am now faced with the task of dressing myself appropriately. The past years of sketching in pastures and city streets have hardly required me to have formal attire at hand. There is no time to have a gown made, but Princess Margit has most graciously loaned me a crimson gown of silk brocade with very simple lines, exactly to my taste, as well as satin slippers and a necklace with many strands of pearls. She is kind enough to say that the ensemble complements my dark hair and eyes, and suits me perfectly.

*****

October 28, 1897
(The next week)

Budapest, Hungary

My visit to the Hungarian Royal Opera House in Budapest on the arm of Count Ferenc Blaskovits is the stuff of fairy tales. We are conveyed down the glittering streets of the fine old city in a carriage and four. The opera house, with its marble pillars and frescoed, gilded arches, could be an art museum. Count Blaskovits does not leave my side, unless to bring me a glass of champagne, or to find one of his friends to introduce me. We enter our box, and the view could not be better. The opera is mesmerizing, but almost too much for my senses to take in all at once—orchestra, voice, choreography, sets, and costumes. When intermission arrives, I am giddy and a bit relieved, but nonetheless I am eager for the second act to begin.

Count Blaskovits does not attempt to converse during the performance, and I am grateful to be left to lose myself in so much beauty. It seems that this is something else that we have in common. As we ride home, he sits across from me, leaning forward.

"Mademoiselle Lotz, what are your thoughts about the opera?"

"Oh, so many thoughts. This is only the second opera I have

attended, and *The Magic Flute*, which I saw in Paris, was so different from *La Boheme* that I cannot compare very well. I can say that I have enjoyed the evening very much. The singing was wonderful, and I would like to have a whole day to study the frescos in the entry of the opera house."

"So you shall. I will escort you there tomorrow after lunch. Would you like that?"

"Indeed I would, but I would not like to take you away from your other guests."

"The duke and *familie* will attend *Masse* with me, and I am happy if you join us. We will all eat together, and *après le déjeuner* they wish to ride. They will not miss us." His smile is sweet, and a little shy. "*Mais dis moi,* what you think of the story?"

"The story of the opera? I think it is a canvas, if you will, for the composer's music and the splendid costumes. It is a simple story. It brings to mind happy Christmas Eves I have known, and tragedies I have known. But it is too simple to make me think. Life does not happen so simply."

"For example?"

"Rodolfo and Mimi touch hands for an instant and are suddenly in love. How can they be? They do not know each other."

"Ah, you are not a romantic then?"

"No, I am not. I have seen too much evil and known too much sorrow to be a romantic. Rodolfo and Mimi like each other, of course—they are both young and attractive—but this is not love. And Mimi's death is not romantic—it is tragic. Do you not think those four romantic young men could have done something months earlier to get her medicine, when they learned she had tuberculosis, instead of waiting until she is dying?"

He throws back his head and laughs. "Mademoiselle Lotz, *vous êtes complètement original.* You are the most interesting woman."

When I was a young girl, I read and reread the story of Cinderella, but not for the reasons one might think. I was not particularly interested in the romance with the prince, or in the magic worked by the fairy godmother to turn mice into horses and a pumpkin into a carriage. The descriptions of Cinderella's exquisite gowns and the splendid palace were engaging but only to a certain extent. My true fascination was with the fact that the fairy godmother and the prince recognize Cinderella for the person she has always been within herself, even though no one else does. When they see her, Cinderella becomes herself in the world. This is something I have always hoped for. It seems that it is something most people want very much, even if they are unaware of it.

Count Ferenc Blaskovits has recognized me tonight, and he has discovered in me a friend.

*****

April 1900
(Two and a half years later)
On the Nile River, Egypt

I am sailing down the Nile on a river barge with a comfortable cabin to sleep in and a shaded deck on its top for viewing the scenery. In the mornings and evenings, cool breezes blow off the river as we sail past lush greenery, colorful historic buildings, and distant barren mountains. Yesterday evening, crocodiles approached the boat and leapt from the water, which was interesting as long as they were far below us.

During the heat of the day, I sleep, and I am surprised that hours of daytime sleep do not disturb my ability to sleep at night. I am afraid that I am dangerously exhausted. My health has been failing and the doctor has ordered complete rest. It is much needed. Egypt is where I prefer to paint and the work I have done here has been very well received, but the climate has not been kind to me. One would think that the heat would be good for my lungs, but they have become steadily weaker. The doctor believes that this is from a combination of humidity from the Mediterranean Sea and the Saharan dust, which is carried into the city in windstorms, settling on furniture and evidently invading my lungs. I have to admit that I have been working too hard for more than two years, and this has weakened my constitution. It seems that the more I work, the more I want to work, so I drive myself without diversion, and too often without rest.

It was a saving grace when my friend Ferenc Blaskovits came to Cairo to paint last year. We saw each other often, visiting one another's studios to see the latest work, walking and talking in the cool of the evening. In some ways, to be with Ferenc is like painting—the more I see him, the more I want to see him.

Sitting on the observation deck now, I sketch the palm trees along the bank. From time to time, I make a study of a camel or go so far as to paint a landscape, but not with the earnestness and effort I would ordinarily give. If I am to recover sufficiently to work again, I must follow the doctor's prescription and do very little until I have healed.

*****

September 1900 (Five months later)

The Imperial Palace, Vienna, Austria

My hope to begin working again soon has been fulfilled to an overwhelming degree. I am greatly honored to be painting several portraits for His Imperial and Royal Apostolic Majesty Franz Joseph, Emperor of Austria, King of Hungary.

I could not sleep last night, knowing that I was to be presented to him today. Earl Miklos Esterházy has accompanied me, since it was he who first showed his majesty my paintings and secured the commission. We have driven here in the earl's carriage and stayed last night at his Vienna house. If he were my own father, he could not be kinder to me and I am very grateful. At the moment, I am also very fearful.

Our carriage stops before the imperial palace with its white stone glistening in the morning sun. A fine bronze statue of horse and rider presides over the courtyard. We are escorted down one very long corridor and then another, and at last seated in a waiting room decorated in greens and gold. As we wait, a terrible thought occurs to me.

"I have not practiced what I will say! How do I address the emperor?"

"You will speak French, I think, will you not? The emperor does not speak English."

"Yes, French. My German is only that of a child."

"In this case you will address him as *Votre Majesté Impériale*."

"*Votre Majesté Impériale. Votre Majesté Impériale. Votre Majesté Impériale.*"

Earl Esterházy laughs heartily as I practice. "The emperor is very gracious, Matilda. You do not need to be afraid."

I am not convinced. "Do I curtsey? A full court curtsey?"

"If you wish, but he understands that you are American. Besides, he will be as charmed as I am with Mademoiselle Matilda Lotz."

A servant opens the door and speaks in Hungarian, presumably announcing the emperor. Through the door steps a man who looks more like a grandfather than an emperor—quite elderly though with an erect posture, great huge white moustaches, and quick eyes that seem to be smiling. He is dressed in military uniform with a row of medals pinned across his breast.

Earl Esterházy, who is the emperor's second in command, makes a low bow, so I execute a full court curtsey to the best of my ability.

"Salutations, Mlle. Lotz. *Vous allez peindre mes chevaux, non?*" the Emperor greets me, asking whether I will be painting his horses.

"*Oui, Votre Majesté Impériale, avec plaisir*," I answer, confirming that I will be happy to do so.

"*Bon*."

The emperor tells me that I will be escorted when I am ready, and that I should ask his servants for whatever I need. The stables? I want to paint the horses where they can move and reveal their natures, but my limited French will not be able to convey this well in so formal a situation. Happily, my patron and friend the earl has seen my dismay and guessed the reason. He knows well that whenever possible I paint animals in the open, and he knows why. He speaks at length with the emperor in Hungarian.

His imperial majesty turns to me, and to my great surprise, he smiles broadly. Now he truly resembles a kindly grandfather. "*Peinture où vous choisissez, mademoiselle. J'avance de très beaux portraits*," telling me that I may paint wherever I choose, and that he anticipates some very fine portraits.

I return his smile sincerely, and curtsey again.

The three horses are the most magnificent I have seen. They are all Arabian, with the finest skeletal structure and eyes full of intelligence. Of the two stallions, one is jet black with a fiery nature, rearing and prancing the entire time I sketched him, and the other is a shade of brown that is very red in tone and has a calmer temperament. The mare is white with a flowing mane, and almost ethereal. Horses such as she no doubt inspired the tales of unicorns.

During the first week that I am sketching the horses, my friend Ferenc Blaskovits arrives at the earl's home to tell me that he has come to Vienna with the express purpose of escorting me to the opera at the Wiener Staatsoper, the Vienna State Opera, which is said to be the finest in the world. He has secured season tickets to Wagner's *Der Ring des Nibelungen, The Ring of the Nibelung*—actually a series of four operas. I am delighted, but not entirely surprised. This time I have come prepared with evening attire.

"I think you will find that this story is not simple, Matilda," he tells me with a smile that brings interesting creases to the tanned skin at the corners of his eyes.

*****

December 10, 1900 (Three months later)

Vienna, Austria

"Brunhilde is the hero, of course, not Siegfried," Ferenc says, as we take our seats in the restaurant after the performance of the fourth and final opera in the series.

"It is interesting that you call her a hero," I say. "Most people would use the word 'heroine' because she is a woman, but her heroism is of a different sort than that of most women. She is a warrior, and she dies for her cause. But Siegfried is a hero, too. The victory belongs to both of them together."

"They have a great love. The tragedy is not that they die, but that the poison makes them to forget their love. Do you understand?"

"I do. Your English is getting better than my French, to my disgrace. Hagen give them the cursed potion because of the lust for power and wealth that begins the whole problem of the ring in the first place. Everyone suffers from it, especially the two who are trying to overcome it."

"Love ends the curse. Brunhilde remembers that she loves Siegfried."

"I am not sure that is the point. When she rides into the flames of his funeral pyre, the world is saved from the evil of the ring. Brunhilde begins as a warrior goddess who does not need a man, and she ends the same way, regardless of her love for Siegfried."

Ferenc sighs and the waiter approaches our table.

*****

April 1905 (Four and a half years later)

Paris, France

Ferenc has come to Paris to paint this spring. We share a love for this majestic city, where artists from all over the world congregate, and for the quaint villages and picturesque countryside surrounding it. Often we ride out into the country to sketch, he the landscape and I whatever animals the day presents me—cows and sheep mainly, but also the occasional fox or horses. When we return, tired and hungry, we eat at a café and walk for hours along the Seine or up and down the hilly streets of Montmartre, talking of our work and our families.

It is a great pleasure to share my work in this way again. I had not thought it would be possible to have such a friend, not since Rosa died. Besides, Rosa's and mine was a different type of friendship—that of a mature woman and a young and inexperienced one, of a great painter and an aspiring student. No matter how much

I learned and grew, Rosa was always far above me. Ferenc and I stand eye to eye as painters, sharing the adventure of our creative lives as my brother Paul and I have done for so long, but Paul is a continent away and Ferenc, I am glad to say, is here.

*****

November 11, 1905
(Six months later)
9 Rue Campagne Premier

My dear papa is gone. I have expected the news for a long while, so the quality of my grief is not a sharp pain, but a deep aching, an absence.

Papa's strength and vigor have been fading gradually since long before Mama became ill, and especially in the seven years since her death. This is not surprising, since they were as truly one as any couple I have known. In fact, I had expected him to die much sooner after she did. He has had a long life—eighty-five years—and a wonderfully creative one, not only in the beauty of his woodcraft, but in the fineness and integrity of his relationships with everyone, especially his children. My main regret, as with Mama's passing, is that it has been so many years since we have seen each other. For so long now we have lived in different realms, on different continents, and rather than continuing to know each other, we have become idealized images for each other—I do not think it possible to be otherwise during so long a separation. I do not say that this is bad or good, but it is not relationship really, though I know our love for each other has never diminished. Now we are separated by a greater distance in realms yet more distinct, but every time I pick up a pencil to sketch or a brush to paint, Papa will be with me.

It is sad not to be with my family to mourn. Joseph and his wife, Amelia and her family, Paul and Gus will bury Papa without me, as they buried Mama. I simply do not have the funds to travel to America, even if it were practical for the funeral to be postponed for such a long journey.

I am thankful today to have my friend Ferenc to lean upon. He has arranged for a Mass to be said for Papa at the Catholic basilica at Montmartre, Basilique du Sacré-Cœur, a grand and inspiring place. Though the service is largely foreign to me, the beauty of it soothes my heart. It is as if it were Papa's funeral. I have dressed in black and worn a heavy veil. Upon entering, we light a large votive candle for Papa that will burn the week through as a symbol of our prayers. The priest mentions Papa's name several times during the Mass in special prayers. When I leave, I feel that the worst of the sorrow has been purged away.

What a friend and brother Ferenc is to me.

*****

April 1910
(Four and a half years later)

9 Rue Campagne Premier, Paris

Ferenc Blaskovits has been in Paris a great deal, and it appears that he intends to court me. I cannot allow it.

Oh, he is without doubt one of the finest men I have known, and in fact is like my dear Papa in his mild, sensitive nature and love of beauty. And, yes, his attentions are charming. Yesterday when I returned home from sketching in the countryside, I found five dozen red roses arranged about my rooms, and the following note:

My dear Matilda,

When we first met, walking in the garden of Tata Castle, I offered you a yellow rose in friendship. Do you remember? I told you then that I would discover your true color. This is that color—Alizarin crimson—deep red of lifeblood, with the cool blue undertones of a lady. Please accept these crimson roses as a token of my highest regard.

Ever your servant,
Ferenc Blaskovits

Of course by now the landlady who admitted him to my rooms has spun a romantic tale about the dashing Hungarian count and the American artist. The neighborhood will be buzzing with it. How annoying when one's private life becomes public.

Who could not be touched by the poetry of his gesture and the sweetness of his message, especially since it must have taken him great pains and some assistance to frame it in English? But it does not escape my notice that in the language of flowers the yellow rose signifies friendship, while the red signifies love.

No, this cannot be. I shall not marry, and our friendship is too important to me to allow for a flirtation.

*****

April 1910
(The following week)
Rue Campagne Premier, Paris

"In Cairo you began to fall in love with me just a little, admit it."

"In Cairo I was in love with the camels and the dromedaries, the Bedouin and the unparalleled light, and I also enjoyed the company of my friend."

"But, Matilda, we are very good together."

"Indeed we are, as close friends and colleagues."

"As more than that. We have shared so much in these past years, almost as if we were married."

"'Almost' is a very important word in that statement, Ferenc. Husbands and wives are promised to each other. Friends are free."

"And you think that you need this freedom to paint, but I do not believe it."

"Well, I believe it, and I require it. I am freely and gladly your friend, Ferenc. I value your friendship above any other, and I value you. Please accept that, and let us not talk about this anymore."

"Very well, Matilda. But I will warn you that I am a very patient person."

*****

June 1911
(One year later)
9 Rue de Campagne, Paris

"Ferenc, my niece Blanche has sent the most inspiring letter and news clipping from *The San Francisco Chronicle.* It seems that Blanche and some of her classmates at the state university are holding a strike of their dramatic production because the director is insisting that they dress and behave inappropriately."

"Indeed, my dear. Her aunt has no doubt inspired her."

I laugh, a little embarrassed and very pleased. Ferenc knows how I care about the rights of women, and it is characteristic of him to say something kind and encouraging at any opportunity. Thankfully his remarks no longer tend toward the romantic.

"I am proud of her," I continue. "Of course, the article has a sensational title: 'Baby Dolls Do Not Like Scene.' To refer to them in this way rewards their courage with further disrespect, but it cannot diminish it. The article says that the young female dancers refuse to fall into the arms of the male chorus, especially since they are required to wear quite short dresses. And the young women have succeeded, Ferenc! The article reads, '…the feature will be dropped for the present, unless the coach is able to bring the men and women of the chorus together.' Rosa Bonheur always said that if women stand together, they can earn greater respect and opportunity, even if only in small ways, even if only one small step at time."

"And Matilda Lotz always says that if we elevate our vision, we can keep company with eagles."

I never said any such thing; he has invented it. Still, sometimes it is a pleasure to let Ferenc have the last word.

*****

August 1913 (Two years later)

9 Rue Campagne Premier, Paris

Escorting me home after dinner, Ferenc drops to one knee and takes my hand.

"You cannot be serious, my dear Ferenc," I say, laughing.

"As serious as I have ever been in my life."

"I am too old for this—"

"You are magnificent."

"I work all the time. I have been ill and tired. I have almost stopped thinking of myself as a woman."

"I have never stopped thinking of you as a woman."

"But my work—"

"Have I ever interfered with your work? Can you think of a single instance?"

"No."

"Have I ever doubted your abilities, or discouraged you, or failed to value your paintings?"

"No."

"Do you know why?"

"You value my work as you value your own. You know what it means to paint as I do."

"Would you ever interfere with my work, Matilda?"

"Of course not."

"So you see we have one mind in this matter. Your painting is prolific now and well received. Marriage now will not change what you have built in a lifetime. And you have been at least a little in love with me for a long while, as I have been so much in love with you, no?"

"More than a little."

"Then we shall paint, and we shall love. Yes?"

"Yes," I answer. "Yes, I will marry you now," I repeat, surprised at myself because my answer seems completely natural and right and I have not one argument remaining.

Ferenc rises and takes both my hands. "Yes?"

"Yes." Then he is slipping a ring onto my finger, a diamond surrounded with a swirl of smaller diamonds and set in platinum. It looks like a constellation.

"You rascal! You knew I would accept!"

"No, my dearest Matilda. I hoped you would accept. I asked my mother for this ring on my last visit, certainly not with self-assurance, but with great hope. It belonged to my grandmother, and I have wanted to place it on your finger for a very long time."

We embrace, laughing at this new, yet somehow inevitable, state of affairs.

*****

September 8, 1913 (One month later)

Basilique du Sacré-Cœur, Montmartre

Ferenc and I join hands to climb the dozens of steps leading to the magnificent white stone church, up and up, toward a new life together. Entering, our eyes soar to the dome above the main altar, where Christ, in gleaming white, extends His arms to embrace the race of humankind. Light streams ruby, emerald, and sapphire through the stained-glass windows. There has just been a Mass, and hundreds of candle flames offer the prayers of the faithful.

We are marrying in a Catholic church because Ferenc is Catholic, and because, like my parents before me, and like the Bedouin I have painted, I am a nomad. The many and varied faithful people I have known have taught me to open my mind, and with them I have learned to find God in each of the many places where I have sought refuge.

We have invited no one, preferring to avoid any fuss, to keep this day our own. I am dressed in a simple, dove-colored suit of light wool with a straight skirt and long, fitted jacket, a blouse of creamy handmade lace, and a close-fitting hat, also dove-colored, with a white ostrich plume. I am wearing my mother's strand of pearls, always her best ornament and now mine. Ferenc has pinned on my lapel a corsage of crimson roses.

Père Martin, with whom we have arranged the ceremony, meets us and leads us to a side altar where, on the spot, he recruits a surprised parishioner and his wife as witnesses. The service is as profound as it is simple. We promise to be true to one another in good times and in bad, to love and honor one another all the days of our lives.

Afterward, we walk down the narrow cobblestone streets of Montmartre and toast with champagne at the Café Beaujolais. The proprietress, a plump, fluttery woman who resembles a pigeon, guesses our occasion, kisses us on both cheeks, and treats us to marvelous *tarte aux champignons*.

And then we return to my rooms, our new home as husband and wife. I am not giddily in love; I am not a blushing bride. At fifty-five years old, I have joined my life to that of my true friend and I am quietly, thoroughly happy. Ferenc and I spend the night discovering one another. I think we shall never stop discovering one another.

*****

June 30, 1914
(Nine months later)

9 Rue Campagne Premier, Paris

I am in my studio preparing a canvas when Ferenc enters looking agitated, the color drained from his face. "Tillie, sit down. I have very bad news."

"Just one moment." I finish smoothing out the gesso on the canvas, seal the container, wipe the knife, and wash my hands, a bit annoyed that Ferenc has interrupted my work rather than waiting another half hour for this visit.

We sit facing each other at the east window.

"Tillie, Archduke Franz Ferdinand and Duchess Sophie have been killed in Sarajevo."

I am stunned. The archduke was the heir to the Austro-Hungarian throne. He was not a traditionalist like his uncle the emperor, but a reformer with great visions for his people. It stirred me to hear him speak while I was visiting the Imperial Palace to paint. "Who has killed him? Why?"

"The simple answer is that a young Bosnian Serb killed him because a small group of Bosnians want independence, but it is more complicated than that."

"Yes, they always say that it is complicated," I answer as hot blood rushes to my face and I begin to shake, "but the fact is that they have murdered an innocent woman and a great man who could have helped them. Do you remember how he spoke about transforming the Hapsburg Empire into the United States of Great Austria? That beautiful map he created? Instead of letting someone with dreams and power help them, they have killed him. Now they will have no one to help them, and it serves them right." Tears choke me as I speak. I did not know I had so much anger.

"If only this were all, but it seems that much worse will happen. Tillie, we may need to leave Paris."

"No! Why?"

"It is complicated."

"That word again!"

"Tillie, my dear, take a few breaths. This makes you upset but we need to discuss it. I received the news of the assassination last evening, and I have spent a night without sleep considering the situation. I do not like to bring politics into our talks, but now I must." Ferenc goes on to explain, in English when possible and in French when necessary, how international relations have been very strained for a long while. He tells me that even when he was a young man, the intrigue and wrongdoing were very great and this is one of the reasons that he knew he could not be active in the government. The politics now, as then, involve treaties and alliances that can make enemies of countries that have no actual quarrel with each other. France is an ally of the Russian Empire, and Russia is the protector of Serbia. Austria-Hungary angered Serbia some time ago by taking its territories in Bosnia, which means that Russia is angered, as well, and so, possibly, France may be.

At this point I must stop him. "This is so twisted that it makes my head ache, Ferenc. Are you saying that France is now an enemy of Austria-Hungary?"

"Not yet, but they could become enemies at any time, and with this assassination that could be soon. What is more, Germany is Austria-Hungary's close ally. The German kaiser loves war and he is looking for a reason for conflict. He is an ally, but I do not like him or trust him. Germany borders France, and an attack on Paris would be easy."

"But, Ferenc, Paris is our home now. Our community of artists and writers is here. Our paintings are shown and sold here."

"It is not a good home if our lives are in danger, Tillie."

"What do you think we should do?"

"We could move to Hungary."

"To Tata?"

"Yes, to my mother's estate, or if you prefer it, to Earl Miklos's estate."

"But what is there for us in Hungary? Is that not the life you left behind to become a painter?"

"I understand. Hungary is my home, but it is not yours. I agree, too, that our artistic life there would be a poor shadow of what it is here. But I think we would be safe. There is little to interest an enemy in the small city of Tata—no government to speak of, little wealth, no strategic location."

"Ha! I think the same could have been said of my home in Franklin, Tennessee, shortly before it became a battlefield."

"My Tillie, such horrible memories you have. But this is not civil war. I think the battles will be elsewhere."

"Is there anywhere else we could go, Ferenc? What about Africa? Is there likely to be fighting there?" My emotions are becoming calmer as we work to solve this problem. I can see that Ferenc is very concerned, and it is becoming clear to me that we have to leave Paris.

"Fighting in Africa is possible—the Ottoman Empire could get involved, but it is not involved now."

"Is it likely to become involved?"

"I cannot say. But you would much rather go to Africa than to Hungary, no? You like it there so much. I do, as well, especially Algiers. I had a wonderful childhood there. We could speak French. There are almost as many French in Algiers as in Paris, and many Americans, as well. You have always liked that."

"We could live there inexpensively, even if we are not selling many paintings. It would be good to paint there again, Ferenc, would it not?"

"It would. We are decided then. I will write to some people today about a house. But we will need to begin to pack immediately, Tillie. Try not to bring too much.

*****

July 1914 (Two weeks later)

9 Rue de Campagne Premier, Paris

I am looking helplessly around our comfortable rooms at all our special things. Without a doubt it is a blessing to be an artist, but it is also a burden, literally. Ferenc and I see things in a more intense way than most, so we develop a kind of appreciation for a chair, a book, or a vase that is so personal it may be called a form of love. To complicate this, so many of our belongings are connected with people we love, some of whom we will not see again in this life. And now "they," whoever "they" are—those powers who do not know what love is—have gone to war again. Now this beautiful city may become a battleground, even as once my home in Franklin became a battleground, and we must flee this home, as well, taking only very little of what we love. I have already given away so many nice things—our Limoges china, which would not have weathered the journey; most of our books, many of which were difficult to part with; and most difficult of all, our little terrier Lumi. Our neighbor Charlene will take good care of her.

It is difficult to know where to begin today—what to pack, what to set aside to give away—but I start with what I cannot part with, taking from the mantle the miniatures of Papa and Mama, and wrapping them tenderly in my best silk scarf. Then there is the porcelain music box from my dear friend Rosa Bonheur. She, like Papa and Mama, has gone beyond this world of painful partings, leaving everything behind but herself. I turn the delicate object in my hands, tracing the finely crafted faces and hands of the two lovely women, arm in arm, who decorate it. "They are you and I, *ma chère*," she said as she presented it to me.

Rosa, why would you, who were so strong and resilient, leave me with this fragile memento of our unbreakable friendship? This sculpture will never survive the journey to Algiers. I turn the key on the bottom and listen for the last time to its melody, "*Tristesse*" ("Sadness") by Chopin, one of Rosa's favorites. It is a fitting tune for these times, and for how much I miss her. The music evokes the features of Rosa's face, so firm, intelligent, and kind. She taught me to paint what I see regardless of anyone's opinion, to be strong in the face of criticism and opposition. It has been said of both Rosa and me that we paint like men, but that is not so. We both have painted as people who portray what they see and do not sentimentalize. This makes us not men, but courageous and forthright women.

I resolve to paint Rosa from memory while I am in Algiers. Then I carefully wrap the porcelain music box in tissue to give to *L'Alliance Internationale des Femmes*, the women's group Rosa always supported. Though she has been gone from this world for only fourteen years, Rosa has become so famous that anything belonging to her should bring this organization quite a sum toward establishing the rights of women to work and act in the world, and this Rosa cared about perhaps just as much as painting.

*****

June 1883 (Thirty-one years earlier)

The Paris Salon

For the first time, I am showing at the prestigious Paris Salon my painting of the two dogs, "Ronflo and Rough." I am confident that the painting is good. The *San Francisco Bulletin* has written a favorable review quoting from a Paris correspondent with the *Baltimore Sun*, and Papa and Mama are so proud they have bought every copy they could lay hands on.

I am not surprised to be here, but I am surely out of place. Not only am I a woman, the only woman in my class at *L'Académie de Peinture de Paris*, but I am an American, and one with little skill in the French language. I stand near my painting, trying to catch a few words of the viewers' comments. Almost no one speaks to me, and when they do, it is only a polite word or two.

But who is this magnificent figure in black silk, regal in spite of her short, stocky physique, her hair cropped as short as a man's? She is approaching me, and I am afraid that she is going to speak.

"*Mademoiselle Lotz?*"

"*Oui, Madame*," I manage to stammer.

"You are the young American woman who paints the animals *comme vos amis.*"

I think she has said that I paint animals as my friends. "*Merci, Madame*. I paint what I see, and the animals are truly—*vraiment—mes amis*, my friends."

As she removes her glove, I note the prestigious medallion of the French Legion of Honor on her right shoulder. She extends her hand. "I am Rosa Bonheur. I also paint the animals *comme mes amis.* And you shall be also *mon amie*, my friend."

I take a deep breath against dizziness. Rosa Bonheur is one of the most respected animal painters in Paris, in the entire world as far as I know. I have studied her work these three years I have been at *L'Académie.* Rosa Bonheur has just said that she wants to be my friend. I hope that my hand is not perspiring too much as I take hers.

But she immediately puts me at ease. She speaks of her striving to see the animals truly, to render them faithfully, as her father, the realist painter Raymond Bonheur, taught her. But the desire is not enough, she says, nor is the eye alone. One must study the physiology of the animals, in order to paint the flesh and bones beneath the skin. I have heard the stories of how, years ago, she cut her hair and donned men's clothing to be admitted to the slaughterhouses where women were forbidden to enter, how she braved the odors and dangers of the bloody warehouses in order to study the bodies of cows, pigs, and sheep to inform her paintings. I say little, though, but simply listen, letting her words kindle new inspiration in me.

After a few moments she takes her leave, but she is as correct in her prediction as she is great in her esthetics. From that moment forward, in spite of the difference in our ages and accomplishments, Rosa Bonheur is my true friend, and I am hers.

*****

January 1885 (Two years later)

Paris

"Rosa, listen, the critics in America like my painting! *The San Jose Mercury News* says, 'A picture by Miss Matilda Lotz, now in the San Francisco Ladies' Art Exhibition and entitled, *Le Premier Dejeuner*, is pronounced by critics as above criticism, and by far the best picture in the exhibition.' What is more, Rosa, and what is beyond my deserving, they rank me near to you. 'As an animal painter she is rapidly taking rank with Rosa Bonheur.' They cannot understand how far your accomplishments surpass my own, dear Rosa, or know how much you are teaching me, but will you forgive them, and be happy for me?"

Rosa smiles her wide, generous smile that reminds me of Mama's. "*Certainement, ma chère*. You are my *protégé*, so of course they compare you with me, and this gives me *plaisir.* You learn quickly and well, but more, you want with your heart to paint truly. This is your great gift, which deserves every honor they give."

I am silent a moment to bask in Rosa's praise, more rare and more valuable to me than the praise of the critics. But her point, that it is the desire to paint well that merits praise, strikes a nerve. I have now won two gold medals from the Paris Academy, and I confess that this great honor has swelled my heart with pride, especially since I am the first woman to receive these awards. Indeed, my work is good. But I have been given a natural talent for which I must be grateful, and that talent has been shaped by the best of teachers to whom I have been led by the generosity of my patrons and by my parents' faith in me. For all of this the authentic response must be gratitude and not pride, since I am not the author of any of these gifts. What then has been my part but to love that which I see, and to strive, even to struggle, to paint it faithfully? This, and purposefulness, a refusal to be moved in my resolve to paint. Yet it seems that to a great extent these qualities also are the gifts of Papa and Mama, and now of Rosa Bonheur. Now that I have come to this realization on my own, Rosa speaks again.

"*Ma chère*, there is something else. You must see this praise for what it is. The critics see the painting, perhaps, and say that it is good. To their great surprise, they see that a woman can paint. Astonishing! They do not see you. They do not know whether you are good.

"*Regarde.* Twenty years ago I became the first woman to receive the Legion of Honor. It is a great prize, no? But how did I receive it? I was forced to wait until Emperor Louis-Napoleon was away from Paris. And why? Because the great emperor could not bear the thought that a woman had won such an honor. My critics and my country could not resist honoring my work, but they did not see me. They could see only a woman despised by the emperor.

"*Ma chère*, the best teacher will see you not as a young woman of twenty-seven, not as a woman at all, but a painter, one who is and is becoming a painter. The best teacher will see that you are good à un degré, how do you say this?"

"The same word. I am good to a degree," I say a little sadly.

"*Oui.* You are good to a degree, but you must continue to become better."

Rosa Bonheur is this teacher who sees me, of this I am certain, but I am too shy to say so. Instead, I rise from my chair to sit on the rug at her feet, and she rests a hand on my shoulder.

*****

January 1885
(Two years later)

Rosa Bonheur's Home at By

The carriage rattles over cobbled streets and speeds down country roads, past flowering cherry trees bright in the afternoon sun. Life confronts death again, and at this moment it is not clear to me which will be the victor.

I left this morning the moment I received the message that Rosa was declining. Will I be able to see her before the end? I have just lost Mama last November. She passed quickly, without my being able to return to California to say good-bye. It would be devastating to lose Rosa in the same way.

At last I arrive at Rosa's farm, and I bolt from the carriage, into the house, up the stairs, as her maid is calling something after me, something which cannot possibly be important enough to detain me. But when I arrive at the door of Rosa's bedroom, I realize what the message must have been—the darkened room is lit with candles and perfumed with rose incense—the priest is here, administering the last rites. People are standing near the doorway, so I join them quietly until the service is completed.

Anna Klumpke stands at the foot of the bed like a somber statue draped in black. This Anna is the American portrait painter from Boston who has shared Rosa's home for some years since the death of Rosa's lifelong friend Nathalie Micas. Many gossip wildly about the nature of their relationship, but I do not know its personal details. I know only that Anna, like Nathalie before her, loves Rosa and shares her life, and I know that, like me, she is a young woman who must witness the passing of her friend. I, too, know what it is to love Rosa, in our case as the student loves the master. Anna does not cry, but gazes steadily at the figure in the bed.

That figure, always one of the strongest and most vibrant persons I have known, is scarcely recognizable. The compact, muscular body remains the same, since Rosa has been actively painting, tromping about her farm, and caring for her animals right up to the end. But the face is drawn and pale, and devoid of that life force that always illumined a room and commanded attention. All has drawn inside now, as the sap of a tree in hard winter, waiting and, so I hope, preparing for renewal.

In French, the priest asks Rosa whether she repents of the sins of her life. She opens her eyes, nods, murmurs something I cannot hear. It seems she has already given a confession and is now affirming it. Her eyes are watery and only half open. Is she in pain, or simply weak?

Now the priest recites the Creed in Latin and some of those present join in quietly. Rosa echoes some of the phrases; it seems she does not have the strength to recite the entire prayer. Then the Our Father is begun. The priest slows the prayer, as Rosa struggles to pronounce each word. Our Father, I say in my heart, forgive her. She was great in her goodness and in her art and perhaps she was also great in her transgressions. She did not know anything but large thinking and bold living. Surely the beauty she made stands out from the mistakes. Surely not only her paintings will live on.

Now Rosa opens her mouth to receive Holy Communion, a

tiny particle that the priest inserts carefully, no doubt guarding against choking, since she seems unable to lift her head, and finally he utters a blessing, asking that God forgive her and lead her to eternal life.

We all murmur, “Amen.”

“Amen,” Rosa says, surprisingly forcefully. And this is the last word she speaks. No doubt exhausted, she closes her eyes and lies very still, seeming to recede into the blankets.

One by one, people nod or bow to the still figure of the great artist, offer a word to Anna Klumpke, and quietly leave the room. I move into a corner where I can look on her, now sleeping, her breasts rising and falling rhythmically.

Now I can weep, sensing that she is already leaving us and will not return. Does she know that I am here? Perhaps it does not matter, since she is occupied with the greatest work of her life, this final metamorphosis. Will it always be like this for me, standing alone in cold, stony grief while those I love leave this world for one I cannot even properly imagine? But my tears warm me, making the pain more present for just a moment before lifting the stone from heart. I weep for Rosa, for Mama, for Paul. I could not say good-bye to any of them. I wonder whether they can forgive me. I weep for myself, the one who remains.

Then suddenly, out of the second-story window, I glimpse Rosa’s lion, bounding across the enclosed lawn.

*****

Fall, 1872 (Twenty-seven years earlier)

Woodward's Gardens, San Francisco

I am standing fewer than ten feet from a magnificent golden lion. His head is huge and haloed with a golden mane that looks so soft I want to run my hands through it, though I do know that if I did, he could kill me. He regards me calmly; I behold him in awe. He is not as large as I expected him to be from what Paul and I read, but his presence is even greater than I imagined—an intelligent, powerful, and noble presence. I am thirteen years old, and this is my first trip to the wonder known as a zoological garden. I want to draw this lion, but I do not, not today. I cannot take my eyes away from him, not until Paul pulls me off to see more animals.

Woodward's Gardens are very popular and hold many different fascinations. Paul would have spent hours at our first stop, the main house, looking at the paintings and sculptures collected from around the world. I agreed that these are lovely and I would like to return to give more attention to them. Then Mama wanted to visit the conservatory of rare plants and trees. But I could not concentrate on greenery or even on art, jealous of every minute I could be spending with the animals.

The birds wander where they like here. The ostriches with their large bodies, long necks, and tiny heads, are awkward when they walk, and hilarious when they run. The flamingos are the most astounding color, an orange-pink—I pick up a drifted feather to press in my journal. Deer, cows, horses, and sheep roam among the birds as if in the Garden of Eden. But the wolves and bears, and of course the lion, are kept in cages. I suppose they must be, or they could not be here at all.

"They don't seem as happy as the animals we saw in the wild on our journey," I say to Papa. "Is it right to lock them up like this?"

"Is it right? I cannot say, Tillie," Papa answers. "Are you enjoying visiting them?"

I nod.

"Do you understand how dangerous the caged animals are?"

"Yes. This seems like the Garden of Eden, but I know that cannot be."

"Then you have some difficult facts existing together. You like to visit them, we are not in the Garden of Eden, and they are as dangerous as they are beautiful. You will need to think about this."

*****

Spring, 1873
(About six months later)
Woodward's Gardens, San Francisco

I have returned to visit my wonderful lion. Today I am going to pet him.

I have thought about the difficult facts existing together as Papa told me to do, and I have come to some conclusions.

I would like to set the lion free, but of course this is impossible. I would not be able to get the cage open, and even if I did it would be terrible for everyone, including him, if he were to be loose in the city. The authorities would have to shoot him to keep him from hurting people. So he is as well off here at Woodward's Gardens as anywhere outside of Africa, which is where he probably wants to be.

The other difficult facts are that he is beautiful and at the same time he is dangerous. This I can do something about. Our horse Obsidian used to be dangerous to ride, but I tamed him. I looked into his eyes and petted him and talked to him until he trusted me. Then I could ride him.

I approach the bars that separate the lion and me. "Hello, my beauty. I don't know your name, but I will call you Sunrise because that is what your mane reminds me of. Hello, Sunrise. I am Tillie." As I speak, he approaches me. I extend my hand just up to the opening in the bars and he sniffs it, the way a horse or dog would do. His eyes are golden brown and so intelligent. I look into them and he does not break the gaze.

I stand there a long time, telling Sunrise about our family and our animals and how I like to draw, and he stands there listening. Then very slowly, I reach my hand through the opening in the bars, closer, closer until finally I can touch his mane. It is not as soft as it looks, but it is thrilling to touch him, to know him.

"I need to go back to my family now, Sunrise, but I will come back soon. Next time, I will draw your picture."

*****

SUMMER, 1893
(TWENTY YEARS LATER)

Basel, Switzerland

Today I have seen a hippopotamus, a rhinoceros, and a giraffe for the first time. They are all astonishing creatures.

I was recently painting portraits of Earl Esterházy's horses in in Hungary when some of his Swiss guests invited me to their home here in Basel to paint their dogs. Today I have been taken by their entourage to a place of local pride, their zoological garden. Here animals from all parts of the world are on exhibit. Indeed this is a great adventure, though I wish I had the time and materials to sketch.

As much as I want to see these wild creatures, I cannot help regretting that they are on display behind bars. There is something I do not like about the attitudes of the people who do this. For example, today we have been told that we cannot view the Bengal tiger, since he is deemed "too aggressive." This makes me smile, since recently I, too, have been termed by critics "too aggressive" in my painting style, "too much like a man." Why, I wonder, do we engage with a being and then criticize it for its nature? Of course a tiger is aggressive; how could it fail to be so?

The breeze is a delicious complement to the summer warmth. I close my eyes to savor its passage across my hands and wrists, and I lift from my neck the hair that has escaped my chignon. When I open my eyes, it is to see, some ten feet distant, the world of two brown eyes enshrined in a huge head of golden fur—an African lion, always one of my favorite animals, one I first encountered in San Francisco as a child. I meet his gaze and slowly approach the cage. As his eyes search my nature, I speak to him.

"Hello, beauty, hello. Who are you? I am Matilda, beauty."

I take the glove from one hand and slowly reach it toward the bars, wanting, as I did years ago at Woodward's Gardens, to pet this magnificent creature, to bury my hand in his mane. I extend my hand to let him get my scent, I on one side of the bars, and he on the other, talking to him, meeting his gaze, until he is comfortable with me. We continue to meet each other's eyes as he sticks out his tongue to lick the tips of my fingers. By now I can tell his frame of mind, and I inch my hand closer to him, through the opening in the bars, closer and closer, until a cry from behind me breaks the mood. The lion rears his head and growls.

"*Fraulein Lotz! Achtung!* Be careful!" My companion runs up behind me, warning me in German and English. "*Mein Gott!* Take away your hand! *Der Lowe ist gefahrlich!* The lion is dangerous!"

"*Jah, ehrlich,*" I reply. "Yes, indeed. He is too aggressive."

"Excuse, Fraulein Lotz? What is it you say?" My companion, an overly polite young man, is offended at my tone.

"No matter," I reply. Obediently I withdraw my hand and replace my glove. As I walk away, I wonder, if Rosa Bonheur had been here, what she would have to say. I wonder, too, whether this lion is aware that he has been forced from his home.

*****

September 25, 1914
(Twenty-one years later)

Algiers, Algeria

We are making a new home again, Ferenc and I. It has been difficult to leave Paris, that wonderful city of art and culture where we have been so happy, but we left not a week too soon. Yesterday I received a letter from our Paris neighbor Charlene. The German army marched on Paris just as Ferenc feared it would. It had already reached the outskirts of the city by the time it was halted by the French army, with the aid of the British, at a battle on the Marne River. Hundreds of thousands of French and British soldiers died, but almost no civilians. It could so easily have gone otherwise. Charlene wrote to us on the night the fighting ended. Her letter says that it is the middle of the night. The city is frantic. Church bells are ringing, people crowd the streets, and gunshots punctuate the shouting. She says that everyone has been so afraid. It seems that they are safe for the moment but she still cannot rest easily. She says that we were right to leave, and that she would do the same if she had somewhere to go.

Our plan to come here was a good one. Algiers is sufficiently out of the way to be safe from the fighting, and since Ferenc grew up here and knows every corner of the city, it should not be too difficult to get settled. Because it is a French territory, its culture in architecture, dress, food, and manners is an interesting blend of North African and European. I am so relieved that we are here, and not in Hungary. I have spent pleasant times resting in Hungary, but for me to live there would be to exist at the edge of the civilized world.

The physical climate here in Algiers is temperate, with refreshing breezes blowing from the ocean. I am concerned about summer, though. It is said that last August the temperature reached 47.9 degrees Celsius, over 118 Fahrenheit. Ferenc, idealizing his childhood, says that it is necessary only to rise early to work, to stay indoors resting in the heat of the day, and to drink great quantities of cool tea. I am unconvinced, but then I am a more skeptical person than my husband.

Our new home, actually the top story of a four-level building, is small but comfortable, and we have had it scrubbed to a shine. It is high enough above the street to admit good light through its many windows, to protect us from much of the street noise, and to offer a view of treetops and sky. Because we have brought limited belongings, it has been fairly simple to unpack and make the place our own.

The small rooms present a challenge in displaying some of our larger paintings, but we do not mind hanging them, propping them, and leaning them everywhere. My favorites of Ferenc's are his Algerian landscapes because of their harmony and movement. I like his Paris series very much, too, and I think I will look at them often when I miss our home there. My favorites among my own are all animals. In the newer paintings—"Camels Grazing at a Camp" and "Scene *Orientaliste*"—the sky is mainly light, and it casts its many-hued illuminations and shadows upon the animals and objects on earth. Especially dear to me are the drawings I made so long ago from the back of our covered wagon, of animals I had never seen before—"Antelopes," "Bison Running," "Coyote Drinking at a Stream"—and the paintings I later did from the sketches. In "Deer in the Woods," one brave doe looks directly at me, unafraid. The other stares into the distance, becalmed. I am in their environment, in their atmosphere; they accept me, sensing my acceptance. How alive is the woodland around us, how vivid the light on leaves. One of my best paintings, "The Wolf," remains in California with my family. I still marvel at how that wolf stood so still, watching me as I sketched him. But I have here with me my first, humble painting, "Mattie." This I display in a place of honor over the mantelpiece.

I take Ferenc's arm, and for a few moments, I am content to see our paintings in a new home. Algiers has its own beauty, its own charm, and we can be happy here.

Then there is a loud knocking at the door.

"*Ouvre la porte! Nous sommes la police!*"

As Ferenc moves toward the door, we exchange looks of bewilderment and fear. What concern could the French police have with two former Parisians who have come here with all the necessary papers?

"*Bonsoir, officiers. Comment puis-je aider?*" Ferenc says with his impeccable manners, making a slight bow.

The soldiers are not polite. They do not even bother to answer, but push past him gruffly, their brusqueness and ill intent monopolizing the room. Next to my composed husband, they more closely resemble chimpanzees than men. One, who appears to be their leader, takes our papers from the table and put them in his bag. Another rifles through our suitcases, closets, and drawers. A third inspects the backs of our paintings, pulling off the paper finishing, evidently hoping to find something hidden behind it.

I can tell that Ferenc is very angry only by the pallor of his face and the fact that his speech is even more controlled than usual as he demands to know the reason for this search. The police do not respond until they have finished destroying the order we have only just created here. At last, after what seems a long while, one who appears to be their leader addresses, not Ferenc, but me. His features and the deep tones of his skin tell me that he is at least part Algerian, and not simply one of the French nationals who are occupying the country. He speaks good English with a French accent.

"Madame Lotz, this man—"

"I am Madame Lotz Blaskovits, sir, and this man is my husband."

"Pardon. I know your work, Madame. You are a great painter, and you have portrayed the people and animals of this country for the whole world."

I bow my head to acknowledge his regard.

"Madame, pardon, but your husband is Hungarian. He is an enemy of France."

I let escape a rueful laugh. "An enemy of France? We have lived in Paris, and been celebrated in Paris, for many years. If you know of me, how can you not know this?"

"You and he have lived in France, Madame, but your husband is a citizen of Hungary, which is at war with France. He is an enemy of the state. He is under house arrest, and as his wife, you are, as well."

"For how long?"

"Until the war is over. We have not found any evidence to condemn him as a spy, but we cannot allow either of you liberty to act outside our observation."

They cannot allow us liberty—how often must I hear this? Why does no one seem to realize the absurdity of such a statement?

"But surely we will be allowed to leave to transact business, to buy food, and to take some exercise?"

"From time to time, when we are able to spare an officer to accompany you."

"This is my problem," Ferenc says to the commander. "It does not involve my wife. She needs to be allowed freedom to walk and to shop in the normal way."

Still he does not recognize Ferenc. This must be a strategy to subdue and humiliate him—the enemy of the people.

"I will send one of my men on occasion to accompany you to the market, Madame," he says. "Remember, neither you nor your husband is to leave this house unaccompanied. Good evening." He makes a slight bow, and leads the search party out of our house.

Ferenc and I sink into chairs, defeated, emotionally exhausted. It will do no good to argue. We are prisoners in our own home.

*****

March 1915
(Six months later)
Algiers, Algeria

It has been torture for Ferenc to remain helplessly inside our house while the world is at war and his homeland is one of the major combatants. News reaches us seldom, and even letters from our families are seized and read, only sometimes being returned to us. Months after the fact, he has learned that his two older brothers have died in battle, one gassed to death on the Western Front, the other dying on the Eastern Front of "unknown causes," likely dysentery. This leaves Ferenc as the only remaining child of his widowed mother, but he cannot even be certain that his letters are reaching her. He longs to visit her in Hungary, to comfort and protect her, but even if it were not for our arrest, to try to go to Hungary now would be suicide, the cruelest blow to his mother and of course to me.

The physical restraint imposed on us is very wearying. Both Ferenc and I are accustomed to walking daily, in recent years up and down the steep hills of Paris, particularly Montmartre. For six long months, we have seldom walked anywhere but inside this small house. We open all the windows and follow the short circuit over and over, as briskly as possible. Anyone observing us would think we had lost our minds, but that person would not be taking into account the ache of unused muscles or the torpor of a mind in a body that does not exercise.

Roughly once a month, the commander of the police sends us a chaperone as promised, and we are able to shop. The pleasure of these few respites from our monotonous imprisonment is comparable to world travel for those who have their freedom. First, to step from the house, descend the stairs, and stand under the sky and trees delight us. Next, we walk, freely swinging our legs and arms, for at least half a mile. This is no great distance but a fine change nonetheless.

Then we arrive at the bazaar, a city unto itself where we find everything we need to buy and much that we do not. Fabrics of brilliant red, blue, green, and purple jewel tones trimmed in gold are suspended from poles above the crowd and delight the eye as they wave in the breeze. Walls display intricately patterned carpets. Gold and silver jewelry sparkles on tables. Aromas of fresh bread, coffee, spices, and roasting lamb mix with those of incense and rich perfumes. Someone may be playing a drum or a flute. Merchants hawk their wares, but also smile and invite us, offering tea as they show us their items. The great challenge is to concentrate on purchasing what is necessary—meat, vegetables, fruit, nuts, cheese, flour, honey, as well as canvas and paints—before enjoying the show. We try to keep our police guard from knowing when we have what we need until he tells us we have no more time. To be fair, the guards have generally been courteous. Finally, we enjoy the walk home, talking about what we have purchased and deciding what we will sketch tomorrow of all the images the day has presented us.

Arrest has had a further consolation, and an important one at that. With nothing to do but paint, we have painted prolifically, and also well, I think. Adversity has a way of focusing the mind, and to work has been a way of venting anger—so much anger at first—and avoiding crippling self-pity. The ancient Greeks wisely recognized that drama can provide *catharsis*, but in my experience, all the arts are capable of purifying and ennobling emotions. Indeed, I do not know how I could have borne these past months without painting. I do not know how I could have borne most of the events of my life without painting.

******

Early May 1915
(Two months later)

Algiers, Algeria

When we were children enduring difficult times, Mama often reassured us with the words, "This, too, shall pass." Our imprisonment in Algiers appears to be coming to an end, and not a moment too soon. The political climate here is becoming more dangerous as the war progresses. Last month neighbors cast disapproving looks at us as we walked to our shopping, and this month we have not been allowed to go out at all. Not only that, but in November the Ottoman Empire did indeed join the war on the side of Austria-Hungary and Germany as Ferenc had thought it could, and its borders are dangerously close to Algiers.

The French have exchanged us for prisoners held by Hungary. Of course we are relieved. We will leave as soon as possible, within several days, for Tata, Hungary, where Ferenc's mother lives. But our release has strict conditions. We are allowed to bring with us nothing but the clothing we wear. We must leave not only our furniture and jewelry but also our documents, our letters from family members (some of whom are dead), our books. Our paintings. Dozens of them. Every one of our paintings must be left behind.

At first it is unthinkable, and I am in a kind of shock. Ferenc, of course, thinks first of me. He comes to the window where I am staring at the sky, and takes me in his arms.

"Have courage, Matilda. The art is inside you. It is what you see, how you see, and who you have become. You have been fashioned by every painting you have created. You are your great *oeuvre*. You are the work of art."

His words pierce through the armor that has kept me from feeling my grief, and I collapse against him, sobbing for a long while. When the emotion subsides, he leads me to a chair and pours a glass of wine.

"And you, Ferenc, are your paintings inside of you, too?"

"They must be. And less grandly, they are on the canvas, too, and the French police here are not stupid. They will not destroy the paintings, but no doubt sell them. If so, the paintings can be seen by anyone. It is cruel that we lose them, it is unjust, but who knows where our work may travel, or who may benefit by it?"

"What you say is probably true, but I do not want to hear it now. Tell me something else, something better."

Ferenc kneels beside my chair and kisses my hand. "Very well, Tillie. I will tell you that the French will allow me to take you with me, and that is enough."

*****

Late May 1915 (Several weeks later)

Tata, Hungary

We arrived in Tata last week, and have taken a small house on the grounds of what was once Ferenc's ancestral home. It has a red-brick structure with windows that, although not large, are plentiful enough to admit good light. Here we can easily walk to the great house to care for the countess, Ferenc's mother, who now relies on him so heavily. Not only has she lost her two other sons, but conscription has claimed most of the servants, leaving only a faithful few, mostly women and children, to care for the countess, the remaining animals, and the sparse crops.

The countess has been extremely kind to me. When we met many years ago on my visit to her house in Budapest with Earl Esterházy and his family, she was courteously imperious, keeping at a distance from the American painter of animals who is, astoundingly, a woman. Now, since suffering has softened us both, she embraces me as the wife of her only remaining son, and has even requested that I call her *Anya*—Mother. Knowing that we arrived with nothing, she has pulled from the closets any article of female and male clothing imaginable for our use. This has worked out well for Ferenc, whose physique is similar to his father's and brothers', but I have a slighter figure than my mother-in-law, and have some alteration work ahead of me. Thankfully, when I was a girl, Mama taught me well how to take in a dress or raise a hem.

The countess—*Anya*—has also furnished this vacant tenant house where we have chosen to stay with her own furniture, draperies, bedding, kitchenware, and tableware. She would have preferred that we live in the great house with her, and we did for several days after we arrived, but we immediately saw difficulties. Since her husband died many years ago, she is accustomed to making every decision, finishing every discussion with her pronouncement. This is no atmosphere for our young marriage, and Ferenc and I are of one mind about needing our autonomy. It is not as if Ferenc must now assume a high state position, receiving dignitaries in his estate house—the war has changed all that—so he may as well live quietly and paint as he chose to do years ago.

We plan to see his mother as much as possible, even daily, since we are the only brightness on her horizon. Her lavish lifestyle has been reduced to subsistence. All of Hungary is experiencing a food shortage due to poor harvests and the Allied blockade. Of course, she has been one of the fortunate ones, since the stores of food in a house such as hers are able to supplement for quite a while the little that can be purchased, but she has many people depending upon her. She still supports a number of servants—women whose husbands have been conscripted into the army, and children, and in the town, long lines of men, women, and children wait daily to receive the soup and bread she provides.

Ferenc and I have spent the past several days assisting the servants in carrying furnishings to our little house and placing them where we want. Now we are surveying our arrangement of the parlor in yet another dwelling, where yet again we have been compelled to flee. The absence of our paintings is painfully conspicuous, but we do not mention them. Instead, Ferenc puts his arm around me.

"We will be happy here, Tillie."

Ah, happy. Ferenc can simply be happy as Paul could simply be happy. Opposites attract, as the saying goes. I see things very differently. We will surely be sorrowful here, and lonely, and frightened. We may have to suffer here and to endure. But we will be together, which means that, at least at times, we will be happy. And, pray God, we will at last be safe. This reminds me of something the room is lacking, not the paintings that are obviously missing, but something that I am capable of adding.

"Wait, Ferenc. I've just remembered something."

I take my coat from the rack in the hall and my scissors from the sewing basket and rip open the lining of my coat to uncover a small parcel the size of a deck of cards, wrapped in my finest silk scarf, a parcel so small that the French police did not detect it as I fled from Algiers. I carefully unwrap it to find the images of Papa and Mama in an original miniature, my gift to them on their fortieth wedding anniversary, which Paul sent to me after Papa died. I walk to the mantelpiece to display it in a place of honor. This one item that I have been able to bring makes a small corner of this place a home.

Now I can answer, and truthfully. "I will try, Ferenc. I will try to be happy here."

*****

November 21, 1916 (Six months later)

Tata, Hungary

Ferenc enters the parlor with a troubled demeanor and takes my hand.

"Tillie, my dear, the emperor is dead. He died peacefully in his bed last week."

I embrace him, and we stand a moment in silent mourning. This is a sorrow, but not a tragedy. The emperor was in his late seventies, and he was not murdered. I will remember him with high regard—Emperor Franz Joseph, his imperial majesty. He understood the way that I see and paint animals. My portraits of his three horses pleased him so much that he awarded me a generous bonus, and displayed the paintings in a place of honor in the palace. He was a great man, and very kind to me. It seems to be an attribute of many of the very great that they are also humble and kind.

"He was a prophet, Tillie," Ferenc says quietly. "He told your President Wilson, 'I am the last European monarch of the old school.' Now he is dead, and our empire is dying along with him."

"So much grandeur is dying, and so much beauty," I say.

"And yet it had many problems. Its passing makes way for other opportunities, the way that your revolution did when America became independent from England. America became a great nation with a new way of doing things."

My noble husband, the head of one of the great houses of the Austro-Hungarian Empire, is telling me about the benefits of a republic. Perhaps even more strangely, I do not completely agree with him.

"But the Americans also lost their connection with a long history of art and culture, Ferenc. It will take many centuries to create the quality of art, of music, and of literature from which they severed themselves."

"But they will have the freedom to create it if they so choose, Tillie."

"And if they do not so choose?"

"Then they will choose to live as peasants, and would not in any case have appreciated those things they have lost. This is a choice."

Marriage is indeed a mystery. It has taken time and patience, but it appears that now Ferenc can see through the eyes of my experience, and I through his.

*****

December 1917 (One year later)

Tata, Hungary

America, my homeland, has declared war on Austria-Hungary. Ferenc says that it has to do with his country's alliance with Germany.

Of all the trials and suffering this war has brought, this is the hardest to accept. Will my countrymen come here, to my husband's homeland, to kill people? Will his go to mine? How can this end?

Life here in Tata has steadily declined. Thankfully few actual battles have taken place on Hungarian soil and those have been at a distance from here, but our enemies have succeeded in harming us nonetheless.

To begin with, we are isolated. Since some time before this declaration of war, for close to two years, I have not been able to communicate with my family in San Jose—mail vanishes into the air. I wonder about Amelia and her family, about Joseph and Gus, and even more I fear that they worry about whether we are safe, or even still alive. I hate feeling so helpless. At least Anya has Ferenc and me, and we her—family means everything in such times as these. Only two domestic servants remain to cook, serve, and clean for the frail countess, so we help as we can with her personal and business affairs. It would be better for her financially and physically to move to one of the tenant houses, but she will not hear of it, and to compel her would demoralize her terribly. The great lady will stay in the great house, even if it is falling down around her.

Other than Anya and occasionally Earl Miklos who is now quite elderly and frail, we see almost no one. We know no other painters and very few people even with interest in the arts in this small city.

What is of far more grave concern is that we are all very hungry. Steadily hungry and increasingly hungry. I have heard that the stomach shrinks and we want less food when we eat less, and even so we are always hungry. Even the modest harvest we expected this year has been poorer than we had hoped, and the blockade keeps the most basic supplies from reaching us. A cruel war this is, in which one civilized nation attempts to starve the civilians of another. Anya's storerooms are nearly depleted, but she has not stopped sending me to feed the townspeople in the square. As long as the few field servants, along with Ferenc and me, are able to dig in springtime, we have the heartier vegetables—onions, potatoes, and beets—enough to last the winter. The result on most days is soup, sometimes with bread from the precious store of flour. For this, each time I am tempted to complain, I give thanks.

I was serving soup in the town square last week when I saw Countess Csilla Tamás, a friend of Ferenc's family, near the back of the line. I smiled and waved, but she only looked startled and did not respond. I returned to my task of ladling soup and when I looked up again she was gone, no doubt to return home to sleep on an empty stomach because she was so embarrassed. As an American, I think this degree of propriety is senseless, but when I told Ferenc about the incident, he shook his head and said that a woman bred as she was could not behave any differently. She was taught always to hold herself above the people and to serve them.

Regardless of hunger, to be given charity in public was more than she could bear. We made up a box of simple supplies, put it by her door, rang the bell, and left immediately. It was not there when we passed by again.

When I was a girl, I once asked Papa why many of our neighbors in Franklin, Tennessee, had slaves and we did not.

"I have two hands to do work, Tillie. God gave us work to humble us from our ignorant pride, and at the same time to teach us and lift us up by showing us that we, like Him, can create. We do not want to renounce that commission by chaining our brother to do the work that is ours."

Austria-Hungary has never had slaves that I know of, but the nobility were so high and many others so low. Decades before the war, Ferenc walked away from the courtly life, choosing to work with his own hands. I do not condemn the life of the nobility—in fact, I admire its grandeur—but I do not think that I am in accord with it anymore. Perhaps it is good that this system is changing. It seems to have been a great weight on both high and low. Perhaps this is part of a needed change that will take place for many who are not free to live as they choose.

*****

July 1918
(Seven months later)

Tata, Hungary

The Russian royal family has been murdered by revolutionaries, as Archduke Franz Ferdinand was murdered. The Bolsheviks were not content to overthrow the empire. It was not enough that they forced the tsar to abdicate, that he and his family were living quietly and humbly under guard in the country. They took him, his wife, his four daughters, and his little son to a cellar in the middle of the night and shot them. I am sure the Bolsheviks would say that it is complicated, and offer reasons that make perfect sense—to them.

In the newspaper photograph, no doubt taken before the revolution, the royal family is at home, relaxing with one another. The tsarina and the daughters are unadorned in simple white dresses and the tsar and the little son wear sailor suits. The beauty of their faces is burned into my memory—too much beauty for what this world has become.

*****

November 12, 1918
(Four months later)

Tata, Hungary

We are eating breakfast with Anya at the deteriorating great house when a servant brings the newspaper and Ferenc makes the announcement.

"Dear ones, the Great War is over. Germany finally signed an armistice yesterday."

Anya looks from Ferenc to me and back again. "*Qu'est-ce que cela signifie pour nous ici?*"

"Yes, what will it mean for us here, Ferenc?" I echo. It is he who studies the newspapers and talks with Earl Miklos and others endlessly about events and their implications, which have little interest for me. The world has made itself horrible and they cannot fix it. I simply want to know how we all can live in spite of it.

Ferenc nods and answers his mother briefly in Hungarian before turning back to me. When we are with *Anya*, we try to speak French, a language we all understand, but this discussion is too complex for our limited vocabulary, and at eighty-seven *Anya* will want only a simple explanation.

"I think very little will change here in Tata for a long while, Tillie. The empire has collapsed—all the empires have collapsed—and we do not know yet what will replace them. The economy will stay depressed until other systems are in place, and that could take years."

"But the soldiers who have survived will be coming home, and they can start growing crops so that this city can start eating better," I say.

"Yes. The soldiers will come home. They can go back to their fields and start growing crops again or back to their shops and start selling merchandise again now that the blockade is lifted. There will be gradually less hunger here. This, too, will take some time, but it will be possible to progress slowly."

"We are not at war with America any longer. My family and I will be able to write to each other again."

Ferenc gives me a sad smile. "Try to be patient, Tillie. Don't expect much just yet."

*****

Late March 1870
(Forty-eight years earlier)

Nevada, the Forty Mile Desert

"Many people have died in this desert, children, and we must be careful not to follow them." Papa looks intently from Paul to Gus to me. "By now you know the rules of the wagon train and you understand that their purpose is to protect us. We have a new rule now, and it is to be very sparing with water. We will not wash until we reach the Carson River, and that will take us four to five days. We will not be able to refill our water containers in all that time. You will not help yourself to water, but Mama, Amelia, and I will give you what you need. If you feel very thirsty or weak between times, ask one of us, and we will help you as we can. We may come across some water in the desert—you must not drink it. Gus, I want you to tell me you understand this and that you will obey."

"Yes, Papa," Gus answers, wide-eyed.

"Good. Paul, why must we not drink the water we find out there?"

"It is alkaline, like the soil that made some of the animals sick. It would make us sick or even kill us."

"Correct. Tillie, do you understand this?"

"Yes, Papa."

After having lost our twin brother and sister to poisoned water, we are not about to disobey this directive, but there are so many other rules. We must wear hats and speak as little as possible to save our strength and the moisture in our bodies. We must eat only a little, for the same reason, and though our hunger makes it welcome, the steady diet of johnnycakes with sparse sips of water is not satisfying. But the most difficult adjustment proves to be, not the care with water, but the strange hours.

It is not just that the days are too hot; the nights are also too cold, so our travel is broken up into periods of a few hours at a time. We rise long before dawn and travel until midmorning. By this time, the sun is so hot that we must take cover in the wagon and try to sleep. Though by this time we are very tired, sleeping is not easy in full daylight, even when we wrap our coats around our heads with only our noses and mouths free to breathe. Whether or not we have slept, though, we must rise again hours before sunset to continue our journey until it is too cold to go on and we retreat again into the wagons for a few hours of sleep. This we do for five exhausting days.

And yet, the desert holds its own barren beauty. The hills and valleys of sand look pure and otherworldly under the cloudless sky. Sunset, when it finally comes, is magnificent with its brilliant reds, oranges, and golds.

For the first two days and more, we see no animals except the vultures circling overhead. I should not find the sight of them so welcome, since they are surely waiting for us to die, but their circling movement fascinates my weary eyes. I would like to draw them, but it is not possible—Paul and I are too tired, too dusty and thirsty to draw, and besides, we are always either trying to sleep or walking. Only little Gus and occasionally Mama may ride in the wagon during this crossing, since the journey through sand and dust is so difficult for the thirsty oxen.

Then in early evening of the third day, we move toward the hills to avoid the alkali bog of the Humboldt Sink. Now we slow down, going only some five or six miles each day. If we are this exhausted, how are the oxen that carry us forward faring? Some of the families have pulled furniture and clothing from their wagons to lighten them, and their belongings look so sad lying behind us in the middle of nowhere. In the foothills we also begin to see a few animals—long-eared rabbits, snakes (against which the wagon master has cautioned us fiercely), and once a coyote in the higher hills above us.

Papa says that some of the women and children have become sick from not having enough water, and he and Mama take them a small canteen of our precious store. We are all weary beyond describing, and thirsty enough, but we are strong, and with Papa's watchfulness, none of our family has fallen ill.

Finally, as I am wondering how I will be able to walk many more days, the announcement comes—one more day to the Carson River! We start dreaming then, and talking more than we know we should. We will jump in the river, clothes and all—men and women, boys and girls (this last from me and Mama does not object). We will drink the clean, clear water even as we bathe in it. We will splash each other relentlessly (this from Paul) and we will eat our fill of warm beans (Mama's promise) and we will sleep through the whole night until the sun rises (little Gus's wish).

After one more day of pushing forward, all this is exactly what we do.

As the sweet, cold water rushes around me, dragging at my skirts, pouring wonderfully over my arms and shoulders, I am thankful—so thankful—to be alive.

*****

February 1919
(Forty-nine years later)

Tata, Hungary

Most of the soldiers who were expected have arrived home. Of the nine thousand who went to fight, only a few more than half have returned. The families of those who have not returned, and who are not on the lists of the dead, must wait, vacillating between hope and despair.

Not all who have returned are able to work—some are injured in their bodies and others in their minds—but Ferenc is marshalling all of us who can, men, women, and children. We are breeding livestock on the neglected estate, and as the weather warms, we will be able to mend fences, tenant houses, and barns. We will be able to plant the all-important spring crop and fertilize it with hope. This year we will sow corn, wheat, and barley, and coax the neglected apple and plum trees to bear. Even now, the brightest rooms of the great house shelter tiny, brightly green seedlings of tomatoes, peppers, carrots, and beans waiting for the snow to melt so they may go into the ground.

*****

January 1, 1923
(Today)

Tata, Hungary

I will try to be happy here, I said in Tata not so very long ago, just after we had fled here from the house arrest in Algiers. I meant what I said. Was happiness a choice then? Could it be so now?

The fire is settling into embers and Ferenc has dropped off to sleep. I am faced with my own company, and it is not agreeable.

I have been at war all my life—poisoning the waters with my thoughts, wounding with my tongue, no more blameless than a soldier with a gun. With each loss my heart has hardened more—Mattie, Tod Carter, our home, all our homes, the beauty, the visions. Sometimes I painted day and night to escape the conflict raging inside, the fury and the sorrow that became more fury. If it were not for Ferenc, I might not even have a heart anymore, but he, too, has suffered from my anger.

I have been angry at war and death, but I have been angry at people, too, so many people I have never forgiven. If I cannot forgive, how can I be forgiven? The weakness of my body is telling me that my life will soon be over. If I do not come to terms now, then when?

I have been an artist. Papa taught me that to make art is akin to the work of a doctor or a minister—to shine light on the nature of things and to make the heart more whole. If my paintings have ever done this for others, surely someone will help me now.

I look up to the images of Papa and Mama on the mantelpiece, but their faces remind me, as they always have, to lift my eyes higher. To remember that neither they nor I could do good or be good on our own merits.

I do remember. I ask the help to forgive.

*****

April 16, 1865
(Fifty-eight years earlier)
Franklin, TN

"How desperately we need Easter this year," Papa says as we walk toward the church in the early morning chill.

Two days ago, on Good Friday, President Lincoln was shot. Even though some say that he brought the war upon us, he was the president of the United States, and the fact that he has been murdered is terrible and frightening.

We have dressed in our best clothes for the Easter service, but Mama says that the ground is still cold and she has insisted that we wear our heavy coats and boots to guard against a chill. These old trappings of winter feel out of place with the green buds on the trees and the sweet, muddy smell of snowmelt.

The church is a sturdy brick building, with tall steps going up to the door, so I know that I am going someplace important. I love to enter it. The inside is open and spacious, with many tall windows to invite the light and white walls to welcome and reflect it. The center of the ceiling reaches up as if to heaven. The pews smell of fine wood, like Papa's workshop, and the little candles we are holding smell of delicious beeswax that makes me hungry for honey.

Amelia begins to play the tall pipe organ up front—it brings the music inside my body. We stand to sing a hymn:

This joyful Easter-tide/Away with care and sorrow!

My Love, the Crucified/Hath sprung to life this morrow.

I can sing now, but very softly. It is new to have a voice again. "My Love" means Jesus who rose from the dead. But Tod Carter lay in his coffin like a beautiful, pale statue. The drummer boy could have been sleeping—he wasn't even pale like Tod—but he was too still. Mattie's head was covered with blood and the blood leaked out of her until she wasn't suffering anymore. All those men in our house after the battle were hurt badly; many of them were dying and were carried away dead. Jesus died, too. He must have bled like they did, and turned cold and pale and still. Then He was alive again. But Tod Carter is not alive, and the drummer boy is not alive, and Mattie is not alive.

At the funeral, the pastor said Tod is alive because of Jesus rising from the dead. I don't want to say the pastor is lying, but I saw Tod Carter in his living room and he was still dead. Maybe part of him is still alive in heaven, but is it the part that laughed and spun me through the air? And what about the drummer boy who was with the blue uniforms who killed Tod? What about Mattie? People don't talk about animals living in heaven. When I asked Papa, he said that God loves the animals so much He must do something good with them, we just don't know yet what that is. We have to trust, he said. I trust Papa, and I want to trust God, too, because I believe He is good like Papa. But so far as I can tell right now, all the ones I have loved who died are still dead, and all killed by Yankees. Except for Jesus, and people killed Him, too, even if He got to be alive again.

In front of the church is a big wooden cross like the one Jesus died on, but He is not on the cross anymore, and He wasn't in the grave anymore, either—that's what Papa read from Scripture last night before we went to sleep. So maybe Tod and the drummer boy aren't in their graves anymore, either, or even Mattie, though she is a calf.

The pastor walks forward to preach the sermon to all these serious, sorrowing faces. They look tired, as if they have been working very hard but things are not going right. Are they all trying to understand as I am? But the pastor doesn't read about the Resurrection like Papa did.

"...they crucified him..." the pastor reads. "Then Jesus said, 'Father, forgive them, for they know not what they do.'"

There it is again, that same excuse that blue uniform gave when he shot Mattie. The same thing Mama said about the ones who killed our babies. They didn't mean to. They didn't know what they were doing. Can that make such a difference?

The pastor is silent for a long time. Mrs. Carter is crying. Mama is biting her lip. Then the pastor lights a candle and holds it up in front of us. He says, "Christ our Light, who forgives us all, is risen from the dead. He will give us the strength to forgive. He will raise us up to Himself."

And that is all—the shortest sermon I have heard before or since, but it does something amazing. When everyone stands, they sing with power and their faces look bright.

The strife is o'er, the battle done; the victory of life is won;

The song of triumph has begun: Alleluia!

The pastor comes into the congregation, and lights the candles of the people in the front pews, and then each person lights another person's candle until we are each holding light and singing alleluia. Singing, though we have lost so many bitter battles, lost a bitter war. In spite of everything, singing alleluia.

*****

Spring, 1864 (One year earlier)

Franklin, Tennessee

I wake in the middle of the night and go down to the kitchen for a glass of water, but I hear someone talking. It is Mama, kneeling in the parlor with her head bowed over her hands. I can guess what the matter is, so I go to her and put my arm around her shoulder.

"Are you praying for Julian and Julia, Mama?"

"No, child," she says, and her voice is as still and deep as the dark night. "They were innocent babies. I am praying for the ones who killed them."

"How can you do that, Mama? I hate them. I do not even want to forgive them, but even if I wanted to, I could not."

"You cannot stop hating by yourself, Tillie, and neither can I—we are not strong enough. We need to ask for forgiveness. Then it can be given to us as a gift."

*****

JANUARY 1, 1923 (TODAY)

Tata, Hungary

I had forgotten, but now I remember.

I'm sorry, little girl, the Yankee soldier said as I bent over Mattie's body. I did not want to listen, but I heard most of it anyway, and it has never left my memory. He said that he had a daughter and he wouldn't want anyone to make her cry. We didn't mean to, he said. Probably he didn't, probably they didn't, those men brashly carrying out their orders, slaughtering their dinners, not watching where their bullets flew. Those soldiers—those human beings—each a world in himself, each flawed and yearning, like me.

I know now how I will portray the soldier in my painting. He will be wounded, as every soldier and every person is in some way wounded. He will be leaning on his horse, that simpler and more integrated creature that will carry him toward the viewer, out of the framework of the battle, toward a better life.

"Tillie, dear one, what is it?" Ferenc asks, rousing himself from his nap.

Only now am I aware that I have been weeping, perhaps quite loudly, not in sorrow but in wonder. I take Ferenc's soft, leathery hand, warm and dear, and for once I am the one who reassures him. Even as I am experiencing and releasing years of pain, even as I am aware that this good battle is only beginning, I do not need to force myself to smile.

"All will be well, Ferenc. I have begun to take care of some unfinished work just now. No, not the paintings in Algiers. You are right; they are out of our hands. This is something even more important. I have more work ahead of me, but a new year is beginning right now, and I know that all will be well."

*****

Epilogue

Matilda Lotz died in Tata, Hungary, on February 21, 1923. She did not recover her paintings, but fortunately, the world has recovered them. Some are privately owned, while others are in galleries or available for purchase at auction. Five paintings are displayed at her family home in Franklin, Tennessee—the Lotz House—now a museum open to the public. One of these is of a wolf, her earliest known painting, completed when she was only eleven years old.

*****

CPSIA information can be obtained
at www.ICGtesting.com
Printed in the USA
LVHW040011251019
635290LV00005B/30/P

9 781400 308606